SPECIAL MESSAGE TO READERS

This book is published under the auspices of

THE ULVERSCROFT FOUNDATION

(registered charity No. 264873 UK)

Established in 1972 to provide funds for research, diagnosis and treatment of eye diseases. Examples of contributions made are: —

A Children's Assessment Unit at Moorfield's Hospital, London.

•

Twin operating theatres at the Western Ophthalmic Hospital, London.

•

A Chair of Ophthalmology at the Royal Australian College of Ophthalmologists.

•

The Ulverscroft Children's Eye Unit at the Great Ormond Street Hospital For Sick Children, London.

You can help further the work of the Foundation by making a donation or leaving a legacy. Every contribution, no matter how small, is received with gratitude. Please write for details to:

THE ULVERSCROFT FOUNDATION,
The Green, Bradgate Road, Anstey,
Leicester LE7 7FU, England.
Telephone: (0116) 236 4325

In Australia write to:

THE ULVERSCROFT FOUNDATION,
c/o The Royal Australian and New Zealand
College of Ophthalmologists,
94-98 Chalmers Street, Surry Hills,
N.S.W. 2010, Australia

FEDERAL AGENT

When Inspector Charlie Chey leads the F.B.I. operation to capture the notorious gunman Red Heydendahl, Charlie is gravely wounded and Red is shot dead in the ensuing battle. Criminals, watching the fighting, mistake Charlie for Heydendahl and rescue him, then take him into hiding for medical attention. But how long will it be before the criminals realise their mistake and discover that they've saved the wrong man? And then their vengeance will be swift and terrible . . .

Books by Gordon Landsborough in the Linford Mystery Library:

POISON IVY

GORDON LANDSBOROUGH

FEDERAL AGENT

Complete and Unabridged

LINFORD
Leicester

First published in Great Britain

First Linford Edition
published 2009

British Library CIP Data

Landsborough, Gordon.
Federal agent - - (Linford mystery library)
1. United States. Federal Bureau of Investigation- -Fiction. 2. Gangsters- -Death - -Fiction. 3. Mistaken identity- -Fiction. 4. Suspense fiction. 5. Large type books.
I. Title II. Series
823.9′14–dc22

ISBN 978–1–84782–872–9

Published by
F. A. Thorpe (Publishing)
Anstey, Leicestershire

Set by Words & Graphics Ltd.
Anstey, Leicestershire
Printed and bound in Great Britain by
T. J. International Ltd., Padstow, Cornwall

This book is printed on acid-free paper

1

Mistaken identity

A big black auto pulled out of the busy traffic lane and sought a parking place near to the burlesque theatre on Chicago's Michigan Boulevard. The driver snarled things to himself because several cars were already taking up space, but someone at the back growled, 'It'll do. What's the difference, we don't want a seat in the stalls, do we? We'll try right here.'

Another black car pulled in behind them, and then another. Then three cars went past the theatre and pulled in about an equal distance beyond. Most of the men got out.

They seemed to know what they were doing. Some stationed themselves on the sidewalks on either side of the garish, chrome-and-coloured-tile front to the place — brilliantly lighted at this time of night. Others went across to traffic cops regulating the flow along the broad boulevard, and said things and showed badges that brought immediate respect.

A small group of four big men entered the foyer and spoke to the manager and then to the attendants in the hall. And then everyone waited for the fireworks to begin. Cars flowed by outside; patrons came and went.

Half an hour later the big swing doors leading into the theatre sighed as they opened to let out a man and a girl. A man pulling a snazzy-brimmed hat low over his bronzed face, seemingly trying to shrug himself into the obscurity of his grey gabardine summer suit. A big man, who couldn't keep the swagger out of his walk for all his other efforts towards anonymity.

They — those four big men looking at the teasing stills of the forthcoming show out there in the foyer — got a glimpse of him . . . and saw that both hands were dug deep into pockets which were bulky — and not just with fists. They exchanged glances, nodded to each other. And went on looking at the picture on the wall.

One blew his nose. Another big man out on the steps blew his.

The moll on the big bub's arm was chewing gum with a big mouth-widening rhythm. She didn't know a thing. She had dumb blue eyes that evaluated a world in terms of Frank Sinatra, mink coats and getting stinko late at nights. She had a greedy little mind that stuck the word 'Gimme' forever at the end of her tongue.

A gangster's dame, and you can't say worse than that.

But her big, hefty consort was no slouch up top. He wasn't missing a thing. Whenever he saw a guy big enough to be a cop he started pulling safety catches back. And there were four here, and another standing out on the steps blowing his nose. He had a feeling that that nose-blowing wasn't somehow natural.

He walked stiffly towards the entrance, shrugging off his yap-yapping dame's blood-red fingertips. Ninety-nine times out of a hundred nothing happened when his suspicions were roused, so what? He'd go on pulling back safety catches, all the same, at the merest sign of something untoward. The hell, this was one guy who intended to go on living, by jeez. And there had been the hundredth time more than once in his life. Maybe this was going to be such a time again.

But he was puzzled. Who knew he was in Chicago? Only Norm Gauerke and Artie Kadoc, who'd sent for him. But with a mob as big as Gauerke's there was always a chance of something slipping out to the cops . . . or, worse, the F.B.I.

Near to the top of the broad steps that led to the sidewalk, his body went taut. *Now he knew that something was wrong.*

He found himself looking on to a Michigan Boulevard on which no traffic flowed. Michigan Boulevard suddenly without a car moving on its broad surface! There were cops holding up the cars a hundred yards back on either side of the theatre entrance. And the cops and everyone behind were silently looking towards him.

His narrowed eyes came round, realised that now no patrons were approaching the pay box, realised that none were coming out after him . . . they were being held up by uniformed attendants.

And the sidewalk was deserted right below him, cops were shoving their beef against a wall of suddenly apprehensive pedestrians.

'A trap!' his brain hammered. Somehow they'd got to know that he'd be here at the burlesque, waiting for Artie Kadoc to collect him. He was right on time — and they obviously had known what time he had been told to leave the theatre. The blood rushed hotly, crazily through his veins; a near-mad anger inflamed him and his hands started to pull out his automatics.

Then he saw a big guy footing it softly across the soft pile carpet towards him. It was one of the four big men at the picture board. Only the other three weren't looking at the pictures now; they were looking at him, and they all had guns in their hands.

The big guy came across with his hands trailing. He might have had a gun palmed or his hands might have been empty, Red Heydendahl couldn't be sure.

Heydendahl looked at the big guy's smooth, coppery face, saw his lank black hair and narrowed, brown eyes, and at once thought, 'Injun!' He should have known. Red Heydendahl was mostly Indian himself.

The big guy spoke when he was a few yards away. 'You'd better bring your hands out of your pockets, Red — empty. You've got no chance. We're takin' you in.' He spoke softly, but he was a man who meant what he said, Heydendahl could tell.

Back of his mind thoughts were clamouring, thoughts that didn't seem important in a crisis like this, yet which insisted on being heard. They didn't form, not quite.

He was trying to remember something about a cop who was an Indian. Someone ruthless and indefatigable on the trail of a criminal. Now, who was it? Where had he heard the guy's name mentioned?

Only Red Heydendahl wasn't stopping to puzzle things out. Those unformed thoughts tripped through his brain even as he jumped towards the steps, his guns dragging out against the pocket linings.

His mouth twisted in a snarl. 'Try'n get me!' he challenged. Think he was going to let them take him in when his future would be bounded for certain by the voltage they could put through a solid metal chair with head-clamps and leg bands on it? They weren't going to take him alive. There was always a fighting chance of getting away . . .

That's what he thought.

The big, soft-spoken guy rammed forward suddenly, shouldering the dumb blonde into a squawking heap inside a doorway, safe from flying lead. Then he came wheeling round, jumping for the gangster. He was big, but the way he moved he was little short of lightning with a supercharger on it.

Red Heydendahl got his guns working as that massive body crashed into him. He knew one of the bullets went home. It seemed to hit the big guy in the head, for in a second blood was oozing out in a bright red stream.

But the big guy was fighting as if it made no difference. Heydendahl found himself crashing down the steps and rolling on to the deserted sidewalk, that weight atop of him. Women started to scream, and brave men who had been trying to get to the front of the spectators ran like hell for the nearest shop doorway. A cop thought he saw a chance and opened up, perforating a nice string of holes in a card cutout of a fan dancer.

Red kicked himself clear. They were lying parallel for one second a yard apart on the sidewalk. Red's snarling face came round to look into the face of his opponent. Then his guns came up to fire.

The big guy came back with some kicking himself. His left foot arched round and connected. It threw the gun hand back against Heydendahl's chest, and the action triggered off the round in the breach. Heydendahl found a hole in his throat that wasn't good for his health. He started to die, fast.

He was almost dead one second later when he saw his opponent stagger to his feet and seem to fall towards a long, grey sedan. He saw a hand reach out, grab the big guy and tumble him backwards into the car.

He was within half a second of his last moment then he remembered something that he should have thought of a while back. 'Not a cop, not a cop,' he was saying to himself, gasping out his life on the sidewalk. 'Cheyenne Charlie . . . F.B.I . . . .'

Cheyenne Charlie, slickest, toughest, roughest of the Federal Bureau's special operators. Yeah, that was Charlie Chey, product of an Indian reservation, now ranking inspector in the world's biggest crime-fighting force.

And because he had been thinking of cops he hadn't thought of the Indian man-tracker . . .

He was a very dead Red Heydendahl when they knelt, gun in hand, beside him a few seconds later.

By that time the car was away. The cops were caught on one leg, not knowing what to do. They watched it stream down the deserted highway towards the lake shore, then looked at each other. An F.B.I. man stared at the bright red blood and made a guess.

'Hospital,' he hazarded. 'Yeah, that'll be it. Charlie's off to hospital.' Again he looked at the red blood. 'That was arterial bleeding. If it isn't stopped quickly, we'll all stand a chance of becoming F.B.I. inspectors.'

The cop to whom he was talking said, 'Hell, that guy sure moves fast. He was in that car and away before you'd time to say, 'Red Heydendahl . . . corpse'.'

Or even, the G-man thought, the word 'hospital'. And he stopped to look after that big grey car, because his alert mind refused somehow to be satisfied. Something didn't fit somehow. He went to where the G-men were standing around the corpse. There was another F.B.I. man measuring some marks on the sidewalk. The G-man said, 'Look, did we have a grey sedan in our party?'

The Fed with the tape paused, then looked up. 'No. All black. Why?'

The G-man looked into the distance after the grey sedan.

'There's something here I don't get,' he murmured. 'And why should Cheyennne roar off to a hospital when he knew we had a surgeon waiting round the corner with an ambulance?'

At which moment, stretcher bearers came running up, along with the police surgeon and his assistant. Some Feds were coming down the steps with the gangster's moll. She saw the blood and the corpse and yapped brightly, 'Someb'dy sure got hurt!' Then she recognised Red Heydendahl, thought for a moment and decided that the time was appropriate for a display of hysterics. She got nicely wound up, and that was unfortunate, because it wasn't for well over an hour before she responded to questioning by saying, 'We were gonna be picked up by a grey sedan. That's how it was to be arranged.'

A few minutes before this enlightening remark, something had happened to make the jubilant G-men roar with delight up in their Chicago headquarters. The Press had slipped up about this case — badly.

The Press gave the F.B.I. too much criticism for any real love to exist between them, so when the G-men saw the headlines in that special edition, they were delighted.

'Breed Gangster Fights Way Out of

Trap,' their astonished eyes read. And then it went on, 'Surrounded by picked men of the F.B.I. Red Heydendahl, Frisco strong-arm mobster, today shot his way to freedom when trapped at the Michigan Burlesque Theatre, Michigan Boulevard. In the battle, one G-man is believed to have been killed.'

Fed-man Joe Hencke roared his head off. 'Boy, will they go green when they hear what a mistake they've made! This'll teach 'em not to go reaching for the first phone when anything breaks, instead of checking up on facts.'

He got through to the editor. He put acid into his mirth and gave the guy hell for five minutes. When he'd finished he put the phone down with satisfaction. 'I've wanted to get even with those guys for a long time,' he said.

The G-man who had been uncertain about that grey sedan came in just then. He was an intelligent husky, and he didn't let much go by him. He was still wrestling with that grey sedan matter.

He sat down, didn't say anything for half a minute, then cut into the talk with the remark, 'I can't find Cheyenne Charlie. Any of you guys know where he'll be?'

It didn't register for seconds, and he had to repeat his question again before they got their thoughts around to the absent Charlie Chey, special operator — the man who had tracked Mobster Heydendahl from the Pacific coast to Chicago.

Joe Hencke said, 'The hell, we're forgetting the man of the moment. Sure, where's Charlie? I thought he'd be in some hospital somewhere getting plaster on that big ugly pan of his.'

The G-man said, 'I've been checking. Charlie doesn't seem to be in any of Chicago's hospitals. I've tried all doctors' surgeries, too, within a couple of miles of Michigan Boulevard, and he isn't to be found in any of them, either.'

'So?'

'I'm thinking something happened to Cheyenne.'

That stopped all talk, damped their enthusiasm following the success of getting Public Enemy Red Heydendahl.

They turned round, those big G-men up in that office, and listened to what the Fed was saying.

'Something's wrong,' he insisted. 'That wasn't a Fed or a cop car that took him away. And I was watching, and I didn't see Cheyenne say anything to the fellar who pulled him into the car. There was a guy at the wheel, and two guys in the back seat.'

One of the F.B.I. men said, sharply, 'Sure, that *is* queer. I went round an' cleared people from those cars parked in front of the theatre. There was no one in that grey sedan when I passed.'

The Fed said, thinly, 'Or maybe they were keeping well down. Maybe they took fright when they saw cops holdin' up the traffic and pedestrians.'

The implication of his words startled them. Joe Hencke said, 'Look, what's on your mind, brother? What's this grey sedan got to do with Red Heydendahl, anyway?'

The Fed came back with, 'I wish I knew.' He thought for a moment. 'Maybe we didn't know enough . . . Cheyenne got the tip-off that Red would be in the burlesque around that time, and we met him there with six carloads of G-men. That's all we knew about things. But I'm gonna make a guess.'

'Yeah?'

'Yeah. That grey sedan was waiting for Red Heydendahl to come out.'

Hencke whispered, 'My God, then they've got Cheyenne Charlie!'

The Fed said, 'Yeah. And the last I saw of Cheyenne he was bleeding to death. You always die unless you stop arterial bleeding.'

Hencke stomped to his feet. 'We're guessin',' he rapped, 'but we'll soon know if it's a good guess.'

He went down to where they were keeping the moll. A woman attendant got rough with her and stuck her head under a fast-running faucet and threatened to hold it there until she snapped out of her weeps and hysterics. The moll thought it wouldn't do her permanent any good so she behaved.

'Sure,' she told Hencke. 'We were gonna be picked up by a grey sedan.'

Hencke stayed a few more minutes with her. No, she didn't know where they were going to be taken. No, she didn't know who owned the sedan. All she knew was that the heat had sent Red skulking into the hills east of Sacramento; then somehow word had come to him that he could be used in Chicago if he'd team up with a mob there . . . he'd be given protection and land in the dough if he came.

So he'd got a car and slipped into Chicago late that afternoon. It had been arranged that Red should be picked up outside that burlesque at a certain time by a grey sedan. Only, some louse-bound scum had tipped off the cops, she opined with a flood of shrill dockside abuse. That was her meal-ticket got shot that evening, and she was feeling sore.

She was very dumb. She yammered, 'I ain't no rod-man. I ain't killed nobody nor done no stick up. You can't do a thing to me, you interferin' G-men.'

Hencke said, 'No? You should study law, fish-brain. Consorting with a criminal is a crime in itself. Slap her into a cooler, an' wake her every hour to ask how she likes it. Can't do anything to you, huh?'

He went back to his office where the other G-men were waiting. He told them what the girl had said, and then they all sat silent and looked at each other.

Then the Fed who had first been uneasy about that car said, 'What're you gonna do now? You know what this means?'

'Yeah. If Cheyenne isn't dead through inattention to a broken artery, he's as good as a corpse right now. He's in the hands of some Chicago mobsters, and they won't be tender with him.'

The Fed said, 'There's just a chance.' Hencke looked at him and thought: This boy's smart. The way he's goin', he's due for promotion any time now. He made a note to recommend Paul Zaharias in his next report.

Zaharias said, 'The newspapers got the story wrong. They thought it was Cheyenne Charlie got croaked, not Red Heydendahl. They've reported it in their columns, and Chicago now believes it.'

'Yeah, an' any moment now we'll have

the first of the razzberries blowin' in on us.'

Zaharias went on, 'Look, suppose the Chicago mobsters don't know it's Cheyenne they picked up. Suppose they think, like those smart newspaper boys, they got away with Red. It gives Cheyenne a fightin' chance while they think that.'

Hencke started to dial. Zaharias said, 'It's a long shot, but you gotta take long shots at a time like this. Cheyenne can't be allowed to go under if there's even a remote chance of saving him.'

Hencke nodded. 'You're right.' He asked for the editor, his face grim. He wasn't going to like the next minutes. While he waited he said, 'Cheyenne's got a better chance than you think. He was put on the Heydendahl case because both he and Red have Indian blood in 'em. They're big, both about a size. Both look Indian. Maybe Cheyenne has got a chance. You bet if he gets one he'll make a lot of use of it. Maybe we'll get inside the Chicago underworld through Cheyenne.'

The newspaper editor was back on the phone. He sounded like a man who expects to have his guts ripped out. Hencke grunted, ‘That story you published. We made a mistake. Your story was right, and we were wrong . . . Yeah, yeah . . . Yeah, that guy was Inspector Charlie Chey of F.B.I . . . Sure, that’s right, Cheyenne Charlie . . . Sure, Heydendahl got away — but we’re after him.’

Those silent G-men in that office distinctly heard the horse-laugh that came over the wire. They sat, sympathetically quiet, while their chief took a verbal thrashing over the phone.

He sat listening, his face growing red at the things that cocky editor told him. After half a minute of it, Hencke replaced the receiver without a word. He looked round at his men.

‘Someday I’m gonna get that yapping little editor and I’m gonna feed him to the hogs — bit by bit!’

Then came an announcement over the intercom system. Someone was asking for Inspector Chey. It was a girl and her name was October Raine and she had just flown in from the New York office of the F.B.I.

2

Celebrity park

Hot blood poured over Cheyenne's face and down his shirtfront. It was in his eyes now, blinding him completely, so that his last vision was of Red Heydendahl rolling over on to his back with death stamped indelibly on his coppery face.

It gave him satisfaction now, in the back of that speeding car, thinking about it. He'd got his man again.

He wasn't in pain, for all the amount of blood he was losing — that kind of wound doesn't hurt, not at the time. But he knew it was a severed artery, knew that the bleeding must be stopped quickly if he were to survive.

He struggled to get his hand up to put pressure on the heart side of the artery. They seemed crowded in the back of that racing, lurching car, and it took him seconds to get his fingers positioned.

He wondered if he had lost so much blood that already he was getting weak.

He couldn't see. Said, 'Where we goin'? Hospital?'

A voice growled, 'Nope. But we'll get a doctor to see your head.'

Cheyenne got weaker. They were a long time rocking along in that car. After a time he knew that he wasn't putting enough pressure on that artery, so he said, helplessly, 'Look, you guys'll have to do this for me. Put your knuckles where I've got mine.'

Even in the lassitude that was affecting him now, he had time to think that these were somewhat hapless G-men, not knowing what to do — anyway not until now doing anything. And G-men weren't usually helpless and knew quite something about first aid.

They stopped in time. Cheyenne was dragged out, feet first, and taken into a room and dropped on to a bed. He felt so weak now through loss of blood that nothing mattered; all he wanted was to keep his eyes closed against that warm, sticky fluid, and maybe go to sleep.

He heard the car roar away, but it didn't seem any time after that before it came back. Then practised fingers got to work on his head, and he knew this was a doctor.

He didn't actually fall unconscious. He was hovering on the edge of it, though, while they bandaged him and then stripped him and bathed him free of his coagulating blood. Vaguely he knew they changed the soaked bedding for fresh linen. Then everyone went out because the doctor said he would be all right if he could get some sleep. One second later Cheyenne was asleep.

When he came to it was daylight and a uniformed nurse was waiting to feed him with something warm and sweet from a bowl. He took it all, weakly, wanting to slip back into slumber again. He was sliding off to sleep as she lowered him on to the pillows. Was almost there when he heard her faraway voice. 'You sure took a toss from that motorcycle, mister.'

Cheyenne thought: Motorcycle? I didn't

come off any motorcycle, did I? Then went to sleep.

It was still daylight, but the shadows were long, when he came to the second time. A white-coated male attendant had come in and must have disturbed him. Cheyenne felt indescribably weak.

He stirred, looked into a pan that had been carved with a can-opener — the rugged kind. Asked, 'Where am I?'

The face gashed open at one side, so that a trickle of slurry words came spitting out.

'Ya'll know soon 'nough, I guess. But I ain't bin told to tell ya, so — ' Then the face creased into what could have been a friendly smile. 'Ya don't need to worry. Ya safe, bud — safe here. An' me, I ain't one of them stooge guys around; I'm one o' the boys, so ya c'n talk safe with me, see?'

Cheyenne licked dry lips, whispered, 'Get me a cup of coffee — a big cup — an' I'll see a whole lot better. God, what I could do with a Java right now!'

The pan slipped open at one side and more words slurred out. 'Ya c'n have a tray of food brought up any time — the doc sez so. He sez there ain't nothin' wrong with ya but what a day in bed won't cure.'

'I hope ya right, bub,' Cheyenne mimicked, but the guy didn't seem to notice and went out.

Cheyenne had fallen to sleep again when he returned, but it was a light doze and he woke to the bub's touch almost immediately. And that coffee was worth waking for. The bub helped Cheyenne into a sitting position, then put the tray before him. He went out before Cheyenne got down to the last bite, and perhaps it was as well.

When he'd finished eating and was feeling fit for another gunfight, Cheyenne noticed that a newspaper had been put under the plates. He didn't feel like reading, because his head was sore and aching now, but some impulse made him shake open the front sheet.

He saw a headline, 'Cheyenne Charlie Goes Out In Boulevard Gun Fracas.' He let the paper fall back on to his empty plates, and if the bub had been there for certain he would have exclaimed, 'The hell, I'm dead — this paper says so!' And that mightn't have turned out to his advantage.

As it was he had nearly read the article through when the bub came back. The paper was pretty acid about the Michigan Boulevard shooting, and rubbed it in, in a way that Cheyenne couldn't understand.

In effect it said, what the heck was the F.B.I. doing? They got a sound tip-off, surrounded the theatre — then let one man shoot his way to freedom against odds that were over twenty times against him.

'One G-man showed courage and resource — the great Cheyenne Charlie, known as the most ruthless manhunter in Federal history. He died in tackling the notorious Red Heydendahl single-handed, while the rest of the Federal party apparently stood around and made no move to help him.'

Cheyenne lowered the paper and sent his thoughts back to that moment: When I'm fit I'm gonna walk into this newspaperman's office an' tell him what I think about him, he mused. They didn't know that the way to catch an armed mobster with as little damage as possible was to let one man go in and do it, while the others stood around ready to let fly if need be to prevent escape. If twenty men pounced, for certain they'd get in the way of each other and some would end up badly hurt.

He was saying to himself: Red didn't get away — couldn't get away, the way things were planned. But then he had read just that in the paper — Red Heydendahl had shot his way to freedom and escaped in a grey sedan!

Cheyenne put his hand up to his aching head. I'm screwy, he thought. That bullet must have done something to my gearbox.

But he knew it hadn't. He knew he wasn't going crazy. In spite of this paper he knew that Red Heydendahl had been a corpse on that pavement before they pulled him, Cheyenne Charlie, into that car. He knew that he, Cheyenne Charlie, special operator, hadn't been killed, as this paper declared. Because, he thought, grinning, it'll be a whole lot hotter than this when I wake up in the next world.

He looked round the neat, simply furnished but colourful room. This wasn't the next world for him — no, sir. He could tell that the walls were wooden, and he had an impression it was like the rooms they had in the motel chalets. A motel? Now how did that add up with the F.B.I?

He went back to his paper without seriously trying to work out the answers to the many questions that were now crowding his active brain. He was reading an interesting paragraph, when the door opened and the white-coated bub with the face like nothing mother owned walked in again for the tray.

That paragraph said, 'Immediately after the incident the F.B.I. put out a call saying that the facts were wrong. Inspector Charlie Chey had not been killed — in fact it was Red Heydendahl who had died out there on the sidewalk. But an hour later they issued a statement that this latter comment did not stand. It was as first published by the newspaper, always first with the news — the trap was bungled by the F.B.I. The mobster was allowed to get away, and in the process a brave and honoured member of the Bureau, Charlie Chey, was killed . . . '

There was more of it, plenty of indignation, for instance, at what the newspaper described as 'a flagrant attempt to bamboozle' the Press. 'But why?' they asked. 'That is what we want to know. Why was a lie issued, only for retraction an hour later? What did anyone gain by telling the Press they didn't know what they were talking about?'

That newspaper editor had gone to town in an effort to get his own back. The things he called the F.B.I. were colourful and only just short of the libellous.

The bub came in. He saw the patient sitting erect in bed, eyes hard and fixed on him. Eyes that had lost their recent weariness, and were alert and suspicious once more.

For Cheyenne was putting two and two together and getting an answer that didn't call for decimal places.

They weren't mugs, down at HQ. That story had been put out for a reason. What was that reason? They knew that Red Heydendahl was very, very dead. Okay, why say he was still alive? What was the purpose behind that manoeuvre?

Then he looked at the headlines again, headlines that mourned the death of Cheyenne Charlie. That was another story put out by HQ. Again, why? Why did they want people to believe that it was Cheyenne Charlie who had got his lot in that gunfight and not the mobster? There was some mighty important reason for it all, and Cheyenne knew it.

When he saw that crooked pan framed in the doorway, Cheyenne got a little nearer the truth. He knew that no man with a face like that could have anything to do with the F.B.I. or with honest employment such as a doctor or a hospital demanded. This guy wasn't on the up-and-up.

So, just that little bit short of the truth, Cheyenne decided to keep his mouth shut before this bub and find out what it all added up to by letting him do the speaking.

But the bub hadn't anything to tell

him. Not much. Just that the boss would be seeing him tomorrow. Cheyenne nodded and said, vaguely, 'Sure, sure, that's gonna be fine.'

Then the bub went out and Cheyenne lay back and promptly fell asleep again.

Breakfast woke him. The bub brought it, along with another newspaper. He didn't give Cheyenne time to read it, but opened it and stubbed the headlines and gave his comments while the G-man got around a good meal.

'They're givin' the Feds hell,' the bub yammered out of the side of his mouth. Cheyenne thought: Yeah, and that's the way you like it, brother.

'They're demandin' an enquiry into the whole thing.' That bub sure was pleased because the Feds were getting, instead of giving hell, for a change. 'You was smart, Red,' he said admiringly. 'I sure gotta hand it to ya, youse a smart guy.'

Cheyenne stopped eating for a second, then nodded and went on again. There was one word in that speech that hadn't gone overlooked.

The bub yammered on, 'Russ Amann

an' the other boys sez they still don't know how they did it — or you, Red. Jeez, they musta sweat pounds. Duckin' down when they see them Feds pull up, then hearin' the firin' and getting' up an' seein' ya tryin' to make the car. Russ grabbed ya — ya owe the guy somep'n fer that.' Cheyenne nodded. 'Then away they go, an' all the cops just stand an' stare with their mouths so big. Kinda surprised, see? Never thought that car waitin' there before 'em could be connected with Red Heydendahl. Reckon that gave you an' Russ an' the boys the break of a lifetime.'

Cheyenne said, 'It sure did.' Then wished the fellow would get the hell out of the place, because he wanted to think this out. Now he knew the truth. He could see how it had all happened. And he thought: If I'm not careful I'll not be lying nice an' warm in a bed like now. No, he'd be stiffening on the floor someplace, like the man they thought him to be. With a bullet in him.

There'd be no mercy if this Chicago mob discovered the appalling mistake they'd made — that they'd brought a well-known G-man to one of their haunts.

The snag-faced bub went out at last, leaving Cheyenne to do some thinking. What he was wondering mostly was, how soon would it be before some member of the Chicago mob recognised him — or at any rate realised that he wasn't Red? Red hadn't worked Chicago ever in his lifetime, so far as Cheyenne was aware, but it was more than likely that some mobster here had worked with Red on the Pacific coast. Must have been, otherwise how could Red have got that invitation to join up with the mob? Mobs didn't invite total strangers; someone must have pinned the personal okay to his name.

Cheyenne had got the tip-off that Red was coming to Chicago while the heat was on for him all along the Pacific coast; he'd even found out the time that Red was to be picked up — and the place, the Michigan Burlesque Theatre. But he hadn't been able to discover the name of the big shot here in Chicago.

Could be Lou Barce and his Stockyard Boys, or Rube Suverkrup's mob, or Hanky Hahn and the protection racketeers. Could be any of them. They'd be glad of a tough gunman like Red Heydendahl.

Well, he decided, he'd find out for himself. First thing was to get out of this joint before his sponsor turned up and saw the mistake that had been made.

He looked round for his clothes. They'd done a good job on them and they were there on a table, cleaned, pressed and neatly folded. Even his gun was there. He went through the pockets. They didn't seem to have been touched, though he had a hunch someone had given the contents the once over — they were the suspicious kind, these mobsters. Particularly he looked to a secret pocket in front of his suit coat, behind the middle button. He kept his F.B.I. shield there.

The pocket was empty.

He sat on the edge of the bed and was aghast. Then, with astonishing haste for a man who had so recently lost a few pints of blood, Cheyenne got into his clothes.

He preferred to die with his pants on, anyway.

He went out. He just didn't understand it. He was in a park as lovely as any he had ever seen. There were tall, graceful trees standing in beautiful cropped lawns that stretched down to an expanse of water that Cheyenne guessed to be Lake Michigan. And set among the flowering bushes were charming wooden chalets. Not flimsy, inadequate things like you got in the fishing villages or at the motels, but well-designed, substantial and comfortable buildings.

They were well detached, mostly screened from each other very cleverly by the contours of the gently-undulating park land. Cheyenne thought they had been built expressly to provide privacy for their occupants, and wondered who they could be and how they fitted in with Chicago crime and mobsters?

He came down the steps of his chalet and walked slowly along the path towards the lake, where some sort of road could be seen. That gun felt comforting under his arm . . .

There was a bathing party down on a sandy beach along the lakeshore, and they seemed to be having high jinks. As he came out of the bushes he was able to see that as many as sixty or seventy people were disporting themselves. This was quite a big colony, whatever the explanation.

He was curious. Deliberately he came down to the beach and tried to recognise faces.

He did. A lot of them.

A fat man who should have known better came running across to retrieve a gaily coloured beach ball. He looked up from five yards away and smiled at Cheyenne. He said, 'Good morning,' nodded pleasantly, then ran back to the party.

Cheyenne stood where he was, the picture of that man's face still before his mind. For he knew that face — who in America didn't know it? It was Vic Plath, one of America's greatest playwrights.

Cheyenne tried to puzzle it out, wondered what connection a playwright had with the mobsters? Wondered what this place was, and how come mobsters appeared to be able to use it freely?

He wasn't thinking so good this morning, he decided, when no answers presented themselves, and he walked slowly across the yielding sand in order to look for other faces.

He saw them — again faces known to most Americans. Celebrities all.

Bev Glotfelty, a talented young musician. Al McKinley, a physicist celebrated throughout the world of science. Ginny Rutherford, whose first book had rocketed her to fame within a year. Ada Grossman who wrote poetry so deep no one understood it, apparently — but called her genius, nevertheless.

And others of similar calibre were there. Brilliant intellectuals, the lot of them; people whose faces were never off the newspapers' front pages . . .

Cheyenne walked back to the concrete road and tried to figure things out. He decided to have a look in one of the cabins. He went openly up to the nearest, opened the door without knocking. An old grey-haired man was sitting at a table, writing. Around him was spread many open textbooks, and Cheyenne saw formulae that appeared to have chemical significance.

Cheyenne looked startled, looked quickly round as if seeking something familiar, then apologised, 'Gee, I'm sorry, buttin' in like that. Guess I must have been thinking of something faraway.' And he went out mumbling that he'd got the wrong cabin.

The old man merely smiled courteously then went back to his work. Outside Cheyenne had to think before he remembered the owner of that face. Then it came . . . Dr. Harry Balk, a world-renowned expert on explosives.

Mentally he threw up his hands. Nothing seemed to fit. Only . . . he was alive, unlike what the newspaper headlines wanted people to believe, and that was good enough for Cheyenne Charlie right then.

The one disturbing thought was that someone knew his secret. That person, whoever it was, who had taken the F.B.I. shield out of its secret pocket.

And yet they had left him his gun.

Screwy! thought Cheyenne, and then stopped dead in his tracks.

Four flat, leathern faces were looking unemotionally at him . . . four men in pulled down hats that brimmed slanted, quick-shifting eyes . . .

Four hoods if ever Cheyenne had seen any.

Then he saw the bub who waited on his cabin, hard behind them. The bub came up swearing, 'The hell, ya supposed to stay put when ya told to. The doc ain't said ya c'n go about yet. The hell, I thought somep'n had happened.' He was bad-tempered and grumbled, and Cheyenne thought that the fellar had had a scare.

'I thought ya wouldn't have strength to get off'n that bed. Gee-zez, if ya hadn't bin around when the boss sent for ya . . .'

He didn't finish his sentence.

Cheyenne thought: Like that, huh? This bub was put in to look after me. Seems I recovered faster than he opined.

He was watching those silent, shifty-eyed deadpans. Trying to fit them into this sylvan heaven . . . trying to reconcile thuggery personified with genius relaxing on a beach back of him.

And wondering what the hell the game was, when they must know him to be a G-man because they'd got his shield from its secret pocket.

The four hoods parted. Cheyenne didn't like it. He had two on either side. Close to him, too, so that he couldn't have done much with his gun if the situation demanded gunplay.

But one of the flat, leathern-faced rod-men cracked into a thin-lipped smile, and words crept out of the side of his mouth . . . 'Guess you owe me quite a bit, Red. Guess you don't seem to know it, though. Me, I got you into that car and away. Me . . . I'm Russ Amann.'

Cheyenne remembered. He too let his face crack open thinly, and jerked out of tight-drawn lips, 'You're Russ, huh? This bub told me what you did. Thanks pal . . . thanks a lot. I won't forget it.' He put a lot of significance into his voice and insisted on shaking hands.

Russ Amann liked it. All these tough

gangster boys liked to get sentimental at times, and this was a good moment. He said, with studied awkwardness, 'Aw, forget it, Red. Reckon you'd ha' done the same for me.' But he liked it, all the same.

Then the others insisted on shaking hands with Red, and it was a very touching moment. Cheyenne quite enjoyed himself. He had stopped trying to figure how a missing F.B.I. shield fitted into things. Everything was screwy, anyway. Maybe that shot to his head had done things to him, and any moment now he'd start running around completely ga-ga.

They were all walking back to the cabin. Russ spoilt a lovely day by saying, 'Rube's up at the house. He came out with us. But Artie had somep'n to do back in town. You'll be seein' him later.'

Cheyenne made his voice sound vague, as if he wasn't altogether listening. 'Who?'

Russ looked surprised. 'Rube an' Artie Kadoc, I'm tellin' you . . . '

Cheyenne jumped in. 'Rube an' Artie? Sure; what was I thinkin' of?' He tried to divert any momentary suspicion by jerking his head back to where the high jinkers gambolled on the beach. 'Guess I was tryin' to get over them guys.'

He saw grins come on to the faces of the rod-men, as if he had touched them on the spot marked, 'Humour'.

One of the hoods cracked, 'Them temperamental louies. Geeze how they c'n live with so much brain beats me.' But he was being sarcastic. He didn't seem to think much of brain that found subtleties in the written word or drama or in the orbits of neutrons, protons or mere clumsy molecules.

Russ said, 'You should hear 'em. They talk. All the time they talk. And all the time they talk about themselves, but no one is listenin'.'

Cheyenne wasn't listening, either. They were turning up the path to the cabin, the bub with the crooked pan leading the way. He was racking his brains for all he knew about Rube and Artie Kadoc.

Rube he'd never heard of; but there'd been an Artie Kadoc on the Pacific Division's files for a long time. Artie had been mixed up in a few things that weren't done by respectable people

. . . he'd been beater-up for the Oakland protection mob, and had had other equally pleasant occupations when the F.B.I. made protection unprofitable.

Then he'd disappeared. Cheyenne thought now: maybe Artie knew Red Heydendahl when he was working the West Coast. Looks like it was Artie gave Red the welcome sign to join up with the Chicago mob while the heat was on in California. Artie was still in town, but brother Rube . . . he was somewhere near by the sound of things.

They went into the cabin. It made the place crowded, but it seemed to give the bub happiness. 'I wouldn't like the patient to be missin' when the doc came round,' he yammered. 'The doc he said for you to stick in bed for some time yet, an' the doc's a big noise now in the outfit.'

Cheyenne put that information into his receptive cells. But casually, to Russ, sitting on his small bed, he said, 'Too bad Artie couldn't get along. Reckon I could do with seein' his homely mug again.'

Russ swallowed the bait. 'Sure, I know how it is between you. You'n Artie was always pals. But Rube'll be along any time now. He's just across at the house.' Russ Amann's flat yellow face puckered in thought. 'You don't know Rube so well, I guess?'

Cheyenne was elaborately non-committal. He said, 'Well . . . ' and shrugged his shoulders as if unable to define exactly the degree of acquaintanceship with Rube Kadoc.

Russ went on being helpful. 'It was five years ago the Kadocs lit out for L.A. Rube came back quick; guess he got homesick for li'l ol' Chi. You couldn't have seen much of him, Red.'

Cheyenne was looking out through the window. Two men were approaching the cabin. One wore the white coat that Hollywood has made inevitable in its association with Dr. Kildare; the other was a lean and gangling man, blue-chinned even from this distance, flashy in his yellow shoes and broad-striped summer greys. The G-man was thinking: I hope to God Rube never met the late Red Heydendahl out in L.A. Because if he did I'm halfway into a wooden box already.

Or maybe into the Michigan's blue waters out yonder, with some plaster of paris hardening in his gullet and a block of concrete around his ankles.

Russ saw the way he was watching and exclaimed, 'Here's the doc.' Then he added, 'And Rube.'

Cheyenne got up from the bed and waited for the door to open. He stooped in front of a mirror that was woman high, not his height, and fiddled around with the plaster at the side of his head as if it irritated him.

He growled, 'The hell, that lead did things to my beauty, I can't recognise myself now.'

Somebody laughed. Then the door opened.

The doctor was cordial. He said, 'You up? You do me credit. I'd have thought that blood-letting would have bedded you for three or four days.' He was tall, thin, small-moustached. The kind of man that thinks himself smart, and goes in for things too big for him and somehow always ends up with a shrill, jaded blonde for a wife, living, in a dark, backroom apartment. Cheyenne had met a lot of his kind.

The G-man nodded, equally as cordial. 'Thanks for all you've done for me, doc. Reckon you just turned off the tap in time, though.'

Then he went forward, boldly, hand outstretched. It was a time for bluff. 'Why, hello, Rube. You don't change much.'

He looked into mean black eyes, saw a pinched, sallow, disgruntled little face staring into his own. Rube Kadoc had a curiously small head, and on top of his long thin stem of a body he reminded Cheyenne of those pin-men that kids draw at school.

Rube's mouth dropped slackly. He said, slowly, 'I wouldn't ha' known ya. *You're* Red Heydendahl?' And the way he said it he sounded incredulous.

Cheyenne gave him the big smile. 'Sure. Look what good livin' does to a fellar.' He slapped his big, barrel chest. 'Guess L.A. built me up mighty fine, huh?'

The moment was tense. Cheyenne knew that the other five men in that cabin were suddenly watchful, taken aback by Rube Kadoc's curious greeting. Only the doctor didn't seem to catch on.

Russ said, 'It's some time since you saw him, Rube. Reckon he's changed considerable, huh?'

Rube's mean, black eyes shifted about Cheyenne's easy smiling face. 'Reckon I didn't but see ya more'n two-three times, but . . . ' his voice became brittle . . . 'but that was enough. I don't reckon a fellar changes all that much even in five years.'

They were all standing now, and curiously they were all facing Cheyenne and all were standing with hands deep in their pockets or tucked down under their left armpits. Cheyenne knew he was in a tight spot. He heard high heels tapping up the pathway to the cabin and wondered how the nurse came to fit into this tangle. She'd seemed a proper nurse, not some dressed up gangster's moll.

Russ Amann jerked out of the side of his mouth, 'Whatja mean, Rube? You sayin' this ain't Red?'

Rube's blue chin came up. 'I ain't sayin' this ain't Red. I'm only sayin' I wouldn't ha' recognised him. He's changed a helluva lot in five years.'

No one spoke. They were all looking at Cheyenne, all waiting for him to say something. For though Rube hadn't said outright this wasn't Red Heydendahl, he had pretty well implied it.

There was a knock on the door. That would be the nurse. The bub went across, opened the door and slipped out. They could hear talking outside.

Cheyenne did the big fellow act again. Smiled bigger than natural and said, 'Well, gee, to hear such things. Now, if only Artie had been here. Now, Artie . . . '

The bub came back, whispered to Russ. Russ straightened and whispered to Rube Kadoc. Then he spoke to Cheyenne, but he still kept his hand under his armpit.

'We got news should please you,' he jerked out of the side of his flat yellow face. His eyes were slit-narrow, watchful for any change of expression on Cheyenne's face. 'There's a doll outside . . . . Red Heydendahl's doll. She came over from L.A. with Red, an' she's the dame what was with him at the burlesque a coupla nights ago. The cops didn't have nothin' on her, so they let her out.'

Cheyenne's eyes slipped from one deadpan to another. There was no emotion on their faces, only a quickened interest in their narrowed eyes. He knew that any second now they might start blazing into him . . . and he hadn't the proverbial cat in hell's chance of getting to his gun before death hit him. So he went on bluffing desperately, hoping for a lucky break, though he just couldn't see one here. He went on smiling confidently.

But groaned inwardly. Letting that girl go just then was one damned big stupid mistake on the part of the police or the F.B.I.!

The bub went across and opened the door. Cheyenne had a vision of frizzed and yellowed hair, flash jewellery, vivid, slinky clothes, nylons and skyscraper shoes. A typical moll . . .

The moll lifted her face to his; he saw white gleaming teeth smiling. Then she ran across to him, flung herself into his arms and cried, 'Red, honey, I bin so worried. I thought them blasted cops had done for you. Oh, kiss me, Red; go on, keep on kissin' me!'

So he did.

After all, October Raine, of the New York F.B.I. office, was well worth kissing.

3

Exposed!

There were loud sighs from the hoods, and they relaxed and took their hands away from their guns. Even Rube gave way with a smile that showed smoke-yellowed fangs.

'Looks like I made a mistake,' he said. 'Maybe bein' shot up at the burlesque didn't help.'

He was being suddenly very agreeable, as if wanting to atone for his previous suspicion, and the thought suddenly came to the G-man that he was slightly overdoing it. He thought: This guy still ain't quite easy in his mind. I gotta watch my step. He'd nothing to go on, nothing concrete; but that Indian instinct, so useful many times in his dangerous life, was alert and giving him warning. Rube Kadoc had nearly accounted for him a few minutes ago . . . he might still do it, for all his apparent friendliness now.

Cheyenne stayed with an armful of G-girl for half a minute. She was gabbling away, one second cooing with love, the next shrilly vociferating dislikes of the F.B.I. and the police, too.

And the things she said. She used words that sounded naughty even to the hard-boiled Cheyenne's ears. He had to grin, listening to her. She was putting on a damn' fine act, he thought.

Then the doc put his foot in it. Said, 'But how did you know where to find Red?' Not with any suspicion in his mind, but just because his tidy brain saw a loose end and he wanted to account for it.

It brought sudden silence . . . and if there can be such a thing as a crashing silence, it was just that.

They were as alert as watchdogs again, in one fraction of a second their bonhomie departing.

And Cheyenne, feeling the G-girl go tense in his arms, knew she hadn't an answer to that one. He looked down into that over-painted oval of a face, saw consternation in those bright, intelligent blue eyes.

Then inspiration came to him. Came in a flash, so that without seeming to pause after the doc's question, he was able to supply the answer.

'When I went out, while back, I phoned her. I knew she'd be at McGuthrie's.' He let himself go into another spell of maudlin fondness. 'Guess I had to tell ma honey I was feelin' all right, and she just naturally had to come out an' see her sugar-pie, huh?'

It was good. Until the doctor said, 'But where did you phone from?'

Cheyenne thought: Durn his pedantic little mind! Why the hell does he have to get everything absolutely sewn up before he lets the matter rest? Because plainly there was no suspicion behind his questioning; he was still intent only on accounting for loose ends.

October Raine's eyes said, 'Get out of that, brother. I can't do a damn' thing to help you now.'

Cheyenne got out of it. He let a look of surprise cross his face and said, 'Where'd

I phone from? Where?' Because repeating a question always gives you time to think. 'Why . . . from one of the cabins down by the beach.'

He thought, 'That's a safe bet. If you have important Johnnies working in these cabins, it's pretty sure they'll be supplied with phones.' Though he didn't remember seeing any wires.

The hoods were looking at the doctor. The doc adjusted his starched white coat and said, apologetically, 'Why, sure. Of course, I never thought of that.'

October's eyes danced and said mockingly to the G-man, 'Lucky break for you, brother, you managed to think of it.'

The doctor pulled stethoscopes out of his pocket. 'The boss is up at the house. If you're fit, he wants you to go over right away. Looks like you're fit, but I'll do some listening to your heart, all the same. After what you went through, some men wouldn't be taking morning promenades only a coupla days afterwards.'

The doc coughed. The cabin was blue with smoke. He said, rather bad-temperedly, 'This is a hell of a fine atmosphere for a doctor to work in.' Cheyenne got the idea the smart Alec liked to shove these hoods around. Maybe it gave him a superiority complex, to lord it over strong-arm boys.

Russ took the hint. 'We'll go outside. See you in a minute, Red. Don't keep the boss waiting.'

'Red' took off his shirt, grumbling that it was unnecessary . . . damn it, he was perfectly fit. Then he lay on the bed, and the doc gave him the end of the stethoscope. October Raine kept up the act by making big mouths behind a lipstick.

The doc was soon through with the routine. After a minute he rose and shoved the scopes back into his pocket. 'You should be dead,' he said. 'But looks like you'll last another hour.' He looked round, his thin face bitchy. October was eating a cigarette fast, and the cabin was getting more smoke into it.

'I'll wait outside with the boys,' he snapped. His eyes looked contempt for the cheap, painted hussy behind the smoke, but he said nothing.

When the door slammed behind him, Cheyenne swung off the bed and crossed to the window. His hand signalled for silence until he saw out. He made a count. The hoods were all in a group along the pathway, the doc moving towards them.

'Okay,' he said, reaching for his shirt. 'I thought maybe someone might be standing outside, tryin' to get an earful. That guy Kadoc isn't completely satisfied, I guess.'

October threw down her cigarette and relaxed with a sigh. 'Boy, was that some moment! When the doc asked that question, I sure thought fireworks were about to blow off . . . and we two would be in the middle of the display.'

Cheyenne grinned, finished buttoning his shirt, then went across and impulsively took her in his arms. She said, softly, 'Go right on doing that, brother. It's comforting for a lone li'l gal and . . . I like it.'

Cheyenne grinned down into her pert face. He hadn't seen her for weeks, but he could remember her and the thick warpaint was no disguise to his eye.

October Raine was quite a stunner. She had intelligence, and it shone in her big, cornflower blue eyes. She was pretty enough to get the wolf whistles when she walked down any street . . . and she had a little, lissome figure that was just 'it' whatever the fashion of the moment.

Cheyenne said, 'When I saw that cheap little doll come chewin' her way through the door, I thought, 'I've had my chips.' Then I saw your face . . . Oh, honey, did it do me good!'

October pouted. 'Cheap little doll!' Then relaxed in a smile. 'Guess that's how I'm supposed to look. They made me up fine down at the F.B.I. These are the actual clothes that Red Heydendahl's moll wore . . . she's got government clothes on right now.'

She looked at herself in the mirror and shuddered. 'I look terrible.'

Cheyenne agreed. 'You do.' Her eyes flashed a warning.

'But you're just fine in my eyes at this moment.' She relaxed and nearly purred. She had a soft spot for Cheyenne. He adjusted his tie. 'Now tell me how you managed to track me here. I don't see how you could . . . unless the moll broke down and told you.'

'Guess again. The moll's been well-trained and can only yap that she wants to see her lawyer. Anyway, she didn't know where they were going when she was with Red.'

'Neither did Red. That's why they made the arrangement for him to pick up a grey sedan outside the burlesque theatre. So . . . talk, sister. How did the miracle occur?'

'They sent your suit to be cleaned.' Cheyenne whirled at that. The F.B.I. sure got on to a lot of things quickly, if they knew that. 'The gang cleaned out your pockets before sending the suit, but they overlooked one thing . . . your F.B.I. shield.'

Cheyenne nodded. 'That was in a secret pocket.'

'The cleaner found it when he started to press the suit. He was suspicious . . . there'd been blood on the suit, and the man who brought it in for cleaning didn't look like a G-man. He decided to make sure, and promptly got in touch with the police. They contacted the Bureau, and the number on the shield said it was yours. So . . . we knew you were somewhere on this estate.'

Cheyenne said, 'I'm goin' to ask a lot of questions about this estate soon. But . . . go on, honey.'

'Joe Hencke decided someone should come on ahead and try to find out what gave around here. I volunteered to come, and they let me because in the end I was the only person who could come.'

'That's cryptic. Give, baby; tell me what that means. The F.B.I.'s got a lot of people in the service.'

'But,' smiled October, 'I'm just about the only person in Chicago who knows you by sight. What's the good of sending someone to look for you if they don't know you in the first place? So they let me come. It was my idea to come out in the guise of your moll. Don't you think it was brilliant?' she asked modestly.

'It was positively mediocre,' said Cheyenne enthusiastically. 'You featherbrain, you shouldn't have done it! You might yet get yourself killed. But I think you're a wonderful girl, all the same, and if you pass out and I get clear, I'll buy you the finest tombstone you can get for ten dollars.'

October said, 'That's what makes me love you so, honey. You encourage a girl a lot. It gives you hope, thinking of tombstones.'

Cheyenne shifted on his suit coat and went to the door. 'Honey, I'd even marry you . . . '

'Would you?' She was suddenly breathless, eager. She did think a lot of Cheyenne.

'Sure I would. Only . . . ' apologetically . . . 'I guess I'm just not the marrying kind.'

October's face fell. 'Blast you, Cheyenne, for raisin' a girl's hopes. But . . . maybe you'll weaken someday, and I'm in no hurry.'

Cheyenne opened the door. 'There's just one thing. How did you happen to be in Chi right at this moment? You're a New York employee.'

October shrugged. 'It was easy. I saw the all-stations alert about Red Heydendahl being on the run, and you chasing him. Then came the hot message from you that Red was heading for Chicago. I thought, 'I haven't seen that homely face for months.' It kinda gets on you, your rugged beauty, you know.'

Cheyenne let his bronzed, battered pan come round to see her.

'That's what you call it, is it? Rugged beauty? Huh, huh.'

'So I decided I was due a vacation, and I hopped the first west-bound plane, hoping you'd be around Chicago when I got here.' She linked her arm with his in sudden affection. 'You know, Chey, all this is unmaidenly. But what's a girl to do when she likes a guy and he won't run after her? You in California, and me a million miles away in New York. Well, that's how it seems.'

Cheyenne rapped out of the side of his mouth, 'On with your act, sister. They can hear us now.'

October's face promptly went vacuous. Her jaws moved rhythmically, though he knew there was no gum in that reddened maw. He heard her voice whine petulantly, 'Aw, gee, Red, after I come out here you get to talkin' to me like that. I ain't been looking at no other men while you've been away. Honest injun. So you don't need to get green-eyed with me, see?' She let her voice shrill up at the last words, and Cheyenne saw covert grins on the faces of the hoods. They knew what it was like, having a dame like this . . . they had them tucked away somewhere themselves, all of them.

Cheyenne growled, 'For God's sake, I don't give a damn, anyway. Only . . . I'll do for any guy I see playin' around you! Watch out, honey, that's all.'

October snapped, 'Gimme a smoke. I'm dyin' for a smoke. The hell, why I put up with your crazy jealousy, I don't know.'

Cheyenne gave her a cigarette, then left her so that Russ could light it for her. To the other hoods he growled, 'Why'n hell we ever bother with women! They always add up to trouble, believe you me.'

Someone said, 'Maybe she got you out of some trouble at that.'

Cheyenne didn't turn. He knew it was Rube Kadoc speaking. The statement was artless, but it had meaning, for all that. Rube clearly wasn't satisfied . . . he was very unsure and for that reason wasn't saying anything outright. But there was still a suspicion lingering in his brain, and Cheyenne knew it was going to stay there until events confirmed or refuted it.

He thought: He'll get confirmation soon, I guess. But he hoped by that time to be able to turn the tables on the gang . . . by that time he hoped to know who was behind the gang, and what pleasure beaches, private chalets and distinguished personages added up to.

They walked through shrubbery until they came out before a big house set like an island in the middle of broad smooth lawns. For some reason the architect had designed the house in classic Greek style, and it was harmonious with Nature, and in this sunshine looked glistening-white and graceful. Clearly it was the residence of some wealthy man.

In a loose little group they crossed the lawns and approached the tall

Corinthian-columned front to the house. They were about to go in when Rube looked back down a curving drive that ended in high, distant gates. Cheyenne quickly looked that way, too. A car had just turned into the drive.

They went into the house, but Cheyenne noticed that Rube didn't follow them beyond the big, cool hall. Russ led the way into a large, high-ceilinged lounge. It was magnificently furnished. He had never seen a room like it before. The carpets and rugs were white, and the upholstery of the dub chairs was velvety black. Colour was infused into the scene by the heavy blood red curtaining that hung like so many long banners alongside the tall, narrow windows.

The hoods looked out of place in such opulent surroundings, only the doctor somehow fitted.

Russ said, 'Some room, huh?' and there was pride in his voice, almost as if he were the owner of the place.

Cheyenne said: 'Some room,' and started to build up in his mind a picture of the real owner. If the boss was the man who had designed this room then he was a man of taste as well as imagination, even though that imagination tended towards the spectacular and the theatrical. He had a feeling the Big Shot wouldn't be that man. Big crooks rarely had taste. More likely the mobster had bought the place just as it was — the rather theatrical effect would appeal to a cheap crook with money to burn.

But that still didn't account for all that genius playing around in the park.

Cheyenne was a long way out.

The bub yapped, 'Take a seat, fellars. I'll go tell the boss ya're all here.' He went out. A car pulled up outside the house.

They smoked and talked, and then the bub opened the door and walked into the room, his jagged pan cracking into a smile. 'Here's the boss,' he yapped.

Several men walked into the room. Four of them. And the boss was unmistakable. Bosses have a habit of showing they're cock of the walk.

Only, this one didn't walk.

They pushed him in on a wheel chair. He was bald and fleshy and flashed teeth that had grown in a dental mechanic's vice. A smiling man, pink, and quick with his light grey eyes.

A man who looked like a male nurse wheeled him into the room, then went out as if having been given some prior order. A girl came into the lounge, passing the male nurse in the doorway.

Rube Kadoc walked in beside the boss. On the other side of the chair came a man with a handkerchief to his face. He was saying, 'I got hay fever. Bad.'

And the boss said sympathetically, 'Boys, Joe's got hay fever. Bad.'

Then he was looking at Cheyenne, smiling a smile so big it was twice the size of the presidential grin. 'Hyar, Red,' he said, and there was affection in his voice. The kind of affection a salesman gets when he sees one of his best customers.

Cheyenne strode over, hand out, and smiled just as big. 'I'm sure glad to see you,' he smiled. 'Guess the party'd be fine if old Artie could ha' been here to meet me.'

He stopped. There was something happening to the atmosphere. But the boss was sitting there, big and pink and smiling so largely he was only an inch short of bustin' out laughing, Cheyenne thought.

And his daughter, as bonny as October, in her way, though dark where the G-girl was fair, brown-eyed instead of blue eyed, rather heavier, rounder. She was looking at Cheyenne with unmixed pleasure . . . as if she liked big men who looked tough and were capable of handling themselves; and she looked the spoilt, possessive kind, as if she got what she wanted. Cheyenne saw the look, and an uneasy thought came to his mind that here could develop a complication.

The doc, sleek and handsome, was looking at the dark girl.

And then Cheyenne looked at Russ Amann . . . and got it.

He saw the snake in Amann's eyes. Narrowed, beady eyes.

Nasty eyes set into slits in that flat, yellow face.

Cheyenne looked at him and thought: Yellow skin. Bloodless. That guy's got poison running through his veins.

And the poison was directed at him, Cheyenne Charlie, right at that moment, he knew. Knew it, but couldn't understand why?

Russ was sitting bolt upright, eyes fixed unwinkingly on the F.B.I. operator. And he seemed to be scratching himself under the armpit, but Cheyenne knew better.

The big G-man let his gaze travel slowly round to the other hoods. They were watching him now, especially Rube Kadoc. Cheyenne saw flat, deadpan faces, unemotional yet somehow registering vicious dislike of him. And all had hands on their guns, he knew.

The atmosphere certainly had changed since the big shot was wheeled in.

The boss got bigger with his smile. Cheyenne waited for the false pegs to drop out, but somehow they stuck. The boss spoke up into Cheyenne's bronzed face. 'Yeah, I guess you'd like to see your old pal Artie Kadoc. Wouldn't he, boys?'

But no one spoke, no one moved their eyes from Cheyenne now. Even the doc and the dark girl got around to the fact that there was a tenseness in the atmosphere.

October had got it long ago. There wasn't a trick that that smart G-girl missed.

Cheyenne shifted his eyes across to her for a second. It seemed that she was desperately trying to get some message across to him with her eyes, but her meaning was beyond him. He looked back at the boss, then saw Russ Amann begin to rise slowly out of the club chair.

October suddenly ripped apart the tension. She spoke, just a little too hurriedly for her words not to sound forced. Cheyenne realised that she was addressing the third hood who had come in along with the boss . . . but he knew in some way she was seeking to distract these mobsters. Maybe, he thought, she can feel this menace, too, and she's trying to open up a moment when I can try reachin' for my gun.

He gave a postscript to his thought: Some good that would be. This corps wouldn't give me much chance of usin' it!

October prattled to the hood, 'That

was pretty lucky for me, wasn't it? I mean, meeting you down at the gate.'

The boss came up with a quick, suspicious . . . 'What's this mean? When did she meet you, Ern?'

The hood shifted his gum. 'She got out of a car down at the gate when I was on duty there. She asked me where Red Heydendahl was.'

'And you told her?' The boss was incredulous.

Ern shifted his gum again. 'Sure. Why not? The dame seemed to know he was here, an' she said she was Red's dame, so I thought it was okay to send her right up.'

The boss was smiling again, big, bald and pink in that invalid's chair. He was looking at October, and Cheyenne wished he wouldn't. The G-man didn't like this cripple; vaguely he felt greater menace from this smooth, smiling man than from the sallow-faced, snake-eyed gunmen.

The boss said, 'But you don't go asking people for Red Heydendahl. Not if you're his dame and you know the cops are looking for him. Not in this State. It doesn't add up. Why take such a risk with a stranger like Ern?'

October looked cynical. 'I guessed if anyone knew where Red would be, it'd be this guy. Look at that pan of his . . . could it belong to anyone on the up-an'-up?'

Cheyenne got the idea that October was deliberately out to rattle someone . . . Ern, it seemed for the moment. Then he saw she was twisting half-sideways, inching her way round so that she could face the window.

When next he looked at the hoods, Russ was playing with a heavy automatic. It could have been casual, but Cheyenne didn't think so.

The boss smiled his big smile and ignored the snarl that came to Ern when he heard the girl's frank appraisal of his appearance. 'Sure, I get you. Birds of a feather, huh? Ern an' Red.' He made a little gesture with his big soft hands. 'Birds of a feather, huh? Like Red . . . an' Artie Kadoc?'

Cheyenne said, heartily, 'Sure, like me an' Artie. Good old Artie.' And he moved a careless pace to one side and that gave

October chance to face right round to a front window.

The boss was playing with him now, and Cheyenne realised it. 'Guess Artie would be right glad to see his playmate again, huh?'

Cheyenne decided to make a stand. His smile was big . . . and false. 'We seem to be going round in a circle,' he said.

'Or weren't we talking like this when you came in?'

The boss leaned forward. Cheyenne caught a movement out of the corner of his eye. Every gun in that room except his own had cleared holster and was lifting to point at him. It made his spine tingle.

'Maybe it's what everyone keeps talking about . . . a vicious circle,' the boss smiled. 'Funny thing is, if Artie did show up, I've got a hunch maybe he wouldn't be as you think.'

Cheyenne said, 'Why not?'

'Maybe because he wouldn't think your name was Red Heydendahl, that's all,' came another voice.

Cheyenne turned. The man with hay fever was putting away his handkerchief.

The G-man saw that face for the first time.

There was some resemblance to Rube Kadoc in it. Then he remembered a photograph he had had to memorise when first he was posted to Pacific Coast Division of the F.B.I.

This was Artie Kadoc. He'd been in the room for the last five minutes.

4

The raid

Cheyenne looked at the guns, then looked at Artie. 'My, my,' he said mockingly. 'I've changed so much even my old cell-mate doesn't know me.'

Artie's sour, 'You betcha I don't,' came back to him.

Russ opened thin lips and asked, 'What're we gonna do with him? He ain't Red. Maybe the Feds did for Red, after all.'

Rube Kadoc snarled, 'I don't like guys that make a monkey outa me. I'm gonna give him his . . . '

The invalid said, 'You'll stay put till I tell you. Before he goes out, I want to know all about this guy. What outfit's he workin' for . . . or is he a cop?' He shot his fat head forward at that. He was still smiling hugely, not a bit disturbed by the exposure of the false Californian gunman.

Russ said, 'He's not a cop. Cops don't have brains enough for a trick like this. He's a Fed. He's gotta go out . . . now!'

Cheyenne felt the quick little surge forward from the gunmen. There was fear behind that movement, fear followed by hatred and a vicious determination to be revenged on the object of both emotions.

But the boss's fat hand came up and stayed them.

'He'll go out . . . in time. But before that I want to get the truth out of him.' The smile was as bright as June sunshine now. 'For instance, if he knows anything about our set up, that would be something of value to us, wouldn't it?'

Russ said, 'Croak him. Feds are dangerous.'

The boss smiled, 'I'm still boss. No, we'll take him to another quiet place, and then you and the boys can practise little tricks on him until he talks. Then . . . '

Cheyenne smiled, 'You're a pleasant son of a so-and-so, aren't you?'

Then October kicked, and even as she kicked she screamed, 'Jump, Charlie . . . jump!'

Cheyenne snapped into action immediately. He jumped head down towards the feet of the invalid. As he started to dive he saw the shoe come off October's foot and crash through the big sheet of window glass. He thought, 'Smart girl. She's got the boys outside.' And then added mentally . . . 'I hope to heaven!'

Then he was rolling round behind the invalid, heard him shout, 'No gunplay. They'll hear guns. Get him and get him quietly!'

But there wasn't much quietness after that. At the invalid's words, Cheyenne rose and started to smash his way out of the room. Somehow October had got across to the door and was already opening it. Cheyenne saw Rube Kadoc jumping across to stop her, and he hit him on the ear and sent the thin-faced gangster smashing to the floor with a sickening impact.

There was a surge of bodies against him, arms clinging, fists jolting into him, rocking him and hurting. He used his strength and somehow drove them off, panting with the savagery behind his blows. There was blood all over the white carpet already. And back over the heads of the flat-faced hoods, Cheyenne caught a glimpse of three other faces.

The doc's. Interested.

The girl's. Wide-eyed and . . . exulting? That's how it looked to Cheyenne.

And back of all was that big, smiling face under that bald, shining head. The boss's.

The hoods came swirling back, and Cheyenne got the taste of blood in his mouth, then smelled it in his nose as a fist smacked down in a chopping blow. Then a bunch of knuckles started some in-and-out business so fast into his right eye that it seemed nearly permanent there.

Yet Cheyenne came out of that ruck again, and did a lot of damage in the process. He'd paid his way through college by grappling in the all-in ring, and the Pit of Pain was now paying dividends in the way of accumulated experience.

Russ Amann went out of the fight with a face as near white as a face can go. He'd been kicking into Cheyenne and the

G-man had at last got around to kicking him back. Once. But there was thought behind the foot, and Russ Amann wouldn't come back for a long time after that experience.

Another hood went down as the G-man concentrated on him and battered at his face until he quit and fell out of the fight.

It provided a breathing space for a second, and then the hoods came swinging in again.

But October had the door open and was shouting from the corridor. Cheyenne lurched into top speed and raced the hoods towards the door.

They were still a couple of yards from it inside that big lounge when they heard the big front doors crash open with a crackle of falling glass.

It stopped the hoods dead in their tracks. The G-man made the door. He saw October round the corner, face delighted, then heard the pounding of heavy feet . . . and many of them.

'The boys!' explained October, and picked that moment to hug the Fed.

Cheyenne just saw the consternation on the hoods' faces, saw them wheel away towards their chief.

'It's a raid!' yelled Artie Kadoc.

'We're sunk!' shouted another hood, and went plunging towards a far door.

Cheyenne saw the heavy man in the wheelchair stop smiling for a fraction, then shake his head.

'We're not.' Cheyenne didn't hear those words but lip-read them. He shoved October away and clawed out his gun. And then he could have sworn that he heard the boss shout, 'You know what to do, Russ!'

Russ went staggering across to the chief in the chair, stood over him. Then crashed the butt of his gun on to that bald head.

The big head lolled forward, blood oozing from a long crack in the skin.

The hoods were racing for that far door. The G-man saw the white-coated doc hustle the girl out ahead of the mob, then got his gun up to fire.

A shot screamed past his eyes. It came from down the corridor. It deflected his aim, and he hit nothing as his finger involuntarily tightened on the trigger.

Cheyenne shoved October on to her back, and went head down to the carpet himself. As he rolled he roared, 'Can it, it's me . . . Charlie Chey!' And the oncoming G-men didn't fire at him any more.

It gave the hoods chance to get out of the house . . . worse, it made the G-men framed targets as they tried to come out through that door, and a stream of lead held them up until other Feds got out farther along through some deep windows.

By this time the group of hoods was across the open lawn and crashing through the shrubbery.

Cheyenne risked an ambush and went flat out across the grass. No lead came. Close behind pounded the other Feds.

They lost the trail once or twice among the trees, and that gave the runaways an even greater lead.

Suddenly Cheyenne found himself running out on to open and just as an engine opened up. A big striped ball came from nowhere and hit him on the chest. A delightful thing in an afterthought so far as bathing costumes are concerned was right behind the ball and collided with him.

He panted, 'It's the wrong time for playin', sister,' and staggered off through the deep, yielding sand to where a motor-launch was pulling out towards the open lake. He had an impression of open-mouthed people of all adult ages and both sexes, then pulled trigger after the fleeing hoods.

The lead screamed and spanged away. More shots came from right behind him as the other Feds came racing up . . . in a moment a fusillade scudded after the crooks.

But that boat went out as if nothing had happened. One moment the bow was down at normal level; the next it was rearing out of the water at the thrust from the screws, threatening almost to topple backwards. In five seconds it was out of revolver shot range, to become a rapidly diminishing black spot in a moving crescent of creamed water.

Cheyenne wheeled, gave an order. 'Alert the coastguards and all police along the shore.' He looked after the launch. 'They might be trying to get across . . . maybe into Canada. Put a Statewide alert on. And get the hover-plane boys out scouting.'

The Fed nodded understanding and went racing back to the house. Cheyenne felt the perspiration stream down his face as, panting, he surveyed the astonished beach-players. He also felt very tired and decided that a man couldn't lose a gallon or so of blood and not suffer some effects afterwards.

He looked at one familiar face and said, 'You're Al McKinley, aren't you? A scientist . . . physicist, I think you call yourself.'

McKinley, lean and hard and unlike the conventional picture of a man of letters, said, 'I am. So what? And who are these . . . er, gunnies?'

'Feds.' Cheyenne was laconic. He never needed to be more when introducing members of the Bureau. 'Just let me do the questioning, though, will you? What are you people doing here?'

McKinley was a tough bird. Maybe he thought there wasn't enough respect in the G-man's voice. He talked back, 'We're guests here. And how long's that been illegal?'

Cheyenne said, 'Maybe it isn't illegal at that.'

'Then why the cross-examination? Do we look like malefactors?'

Cheyenne looked at the bunch. They were a very mixed lot. In fact he thought he had seen much better in the picture files back at the office. He said, 'I'll reserve my answer,' and that made McKinley hopping mad.

Cheyenne turned to Ginny Rutherford, the genius with one book to her credit. 'You're Miss Rutherford. While McKinley's getting over his hurt pride, maybe you'll tell me who owns this place, and what you're doing here?' By the look on the G-men's faces around him, Cheyenne knew he could have got the answers from them . . . they were Chicago Feds, and they'd know who owned a joint as big as this. But he wanted to get these celebrities talking; he just couldn't see how they fitted into the picture.

Ginny Rutherford, timid and uncertain in spite of all her recent acclaim, obliged promptly with the information. 'We're guests of Mr. Gauerke. He — he's a philanthropist who helps artists and talented people by providing them with ideal working conditions.' She waved her hand vaguely. 'Like these.'

Cheyenne said, 'If a philanthropist is a fat guy who sits in a wheelchair, I know Gauerke.'

McKinley came back at that. 'You seem to have met Mr. Gauerke. But in case you're getting too big for your shoes, let me tell you that Norm Gauerke's a powerful man and has many friends who won't let him be insulted. He does fine work, and don't you forget it!'

The man meant all that he said, and his voice fairly crackled as he came out with the last sentence. Looking round, Cheyenne could see the hostility on all the beach party's faces, and he couldn't understand it.

The Norm Gauerke he'd met wasn't a

fine man, was no philanthropist in the accepted sense of the word.

He was a consort of thugs and hoodlums. A crook in a big way, or Cheyenne had never met one.

A man who would have tortured Cheyenne . . . and perhaps the G-girl . . . and then done them to death.

There seemed to be two Norm Gauerkes, he thought, then turned to his rescuers. 'We'll go back to the house,' he said wearily. There was nothing to be got out of these celebrities, he thought. Not just now, anyway. Maybe later they could fit them into the picture.

He looked back at the blue lake. The motorboat was almost out of sight now. He went heavily through the trees after the other G-men. McKinley watched him go and then said sourly, 'That's a smart fellow. Gauerke ought to invite him here so's his genius could have chance to flower.' But he was being sarcastic; he didn't mean it.

A quiet old man who hadn't said anything until then, now spoke up, softly. 'Oh, he's a clever man, all right. While he shot his questions at Miss Rutherford he was watching your face out of the corner of his eye.'

Mckinley looked puzzled. 'I don't get you.'

The quiet old man shrugged. 'It was very clever. It's rather a deep trick. You speak to one person but look at another in order to see the reaction to the questions. If you think no one's watching, you tend to be unguarded about facial movements.'

McKinley said, 'Well? D'you suppose he saw anything in my face? Did I . . . start, or something?'

The older man said, 'I don't know what he saw. But . . . you did seem . . . surprised, didn't you?'

McKinley said, 'Hell, are you playing detectives now? Let's get on with that game.' And walked out of the circle.

Cheyenne and party came trooping across the broad lawn towards the house. October came to meet them. She looked very tawdry in her gangster's moll get-up, and she was limping now because she hadn't got around to finding her shoe yet.

Cheyenne had to say, 'You sure look the part, honey,' and October didn't take it as a compliment.

But he was kidding, and she tumbled to it and they walked into the house arm in arm. An impressionable young G-man came up with her shoe.

October said, 'Thanks.' Then, quickly . . . 'Okay, okay, brother. I can fit it on myself.'

They went into that white-carpeted lounge. Norm Gauerke was huddled forward in his chair, blood still oozing from the crack on his bald head. But a G-man had been attending to him, and as Cheyenne came up he said, 'He'll be all right, so far as I can see. Just knocked out. But we'd better get him to hospital just in case.'

'Yeah,' said Cheyenne softly. 'I wouldn't want that son-of-a-so-and-so to die out on me. He had nice plans for me; now I've got plans for him, instead.'

A G-man . . . it was Paul Zaharias, but Cheyenne didn't know that until later . . . came in with a soft . . . 'You go careful in talking about Norm Gauerke, inspector. He's big . . . really big. He's got pull in high places. That's just a warning.'

Cheyenne spoke grimly. 'That doesn't affect the working of the Bureau. We don't care what friends a crook has.'

'I know . . . but who's going to believe that Norm Gauerke's a crook? Look, you don't seem to know what sort of a reputation Norm Gauerke's got around Chicago.'

Cheyenne said, 'You tell me, brother.' They all stood round Gauerke, drooping in his chair.

'Well, there's never been any hint of scandal attached to his name. On the contrary. Norm Gauerke is celebrated for his philanthropy. Half the beds in Chicago's hospitals were endowed by him . . . he built a wing for the university, has stocked a library, endowed hundreds of scholarships. He must have given millions in his lifetime.'

'No man can collect a million and still stay honest,' cracked Cheyenne.

Zaharias shrugged.

'You're going to have public opinion against you if you start anything against him. Why, even I can't believe he has done anything dishonest or criminal.'

'No?' asked Cheyenne softly. 'Maybe October Raine can give an opinion of him.'

'He's a — ' said the girl unemotionally. 'Okay, I know that's not ladylike, but I learned it in the Bureau, so why shouldn't I use the word? And he's all that . . . and some. He'd have torn us into little bits and then fed us to the fishes, that slob, so why shouldn't I feel poisonous towards him?'

Zaharias said, 'Looks like the guy's developed a split mind in his old age.'

'If it isn't split, I'll split it for him,' retorted Cheyenne grimly. 'Cold-blooded, premeditated murder isn't permitted no matter how many millions you give to charity. Gauerke's got a lot to answer for.'

Gauerke's head came straight up. And he was smiling as big as ever.

Blast! thought Cheyenne. The old man had been foxing them.

Gauerke said, 'Hello. Where am I? Could you give me a cigarette?' Then he relaxed back in his chair, grinning at them. He looked at Cheyenne, and he was near to laughing out loud. ‘I think that’s what people always say after returning to consciousness, isn’t it? I’m playing the part well, aren’t I?’

He was quivering, as if only just able to suppress his laughter. He had a queer sense of humour, that hulk in the wheelchair.

Cheyenne said, coldly, ‘Brother, you’re sassin’ me. Let me tell you it’s dangerous work to kid along the F.B.I.’

‘Yeah?’ That set of pots gleamed up at the Fed. ‘Maybe I like doing it, huh? Maybe I get a kick out of sassin’ you. So what’re you goin’ to do about it?’

Cheyenne’s chin came up toughly. ‘First, you’re going to hospital. Then you’re going into a police cell until you answer a lot of charges. I’m arresting you, Norm Gauerke.’

‘And the charge?’

‘Harbouring known criminals, conspiring to commit a felony, issuing threats against the persons of two citizens of the United States . . . and maybe a coupla dozen other counts.’

Gauerke went right on smiling. ‘You

got it wrong, brother. Those hoods who went off with my daughter just descended on me. I had to do all they said because one was always by my daughter's side, ready to kill her if I didn't play ball. See, didn't they abduct her just now? What do you bet that I don't get a demand for ransom in exchange for her . . . a kidnapping, see?'

Cheyenne shook his head very slowly. 'Your story falls down on several points, Gauerke. There's the evidence of this girl and myself . . . we saw you in pretty close cahoots with those hoods, and they sure weren't threatening your daughter any that I could see.' He thought: Yeah, I remember. When she came into the room she didn't have any escort that time.

Norm Gauerke kept on smiling. 'I don't think your evidence will count for much in court, inspector. At the best they'll declare you not to have understood the situation. At the worst . . . '

'Yeah?'

'You and this girl for some reason are trying to frame me.'

October gasped indignantly. 'Well . . . '

Cheyenne silenced her. His eyes were narrowed and grim. 'You've got things worked out pretty well, haven't you?' He leaned forward. 'Even to a tap on the head to further your alibi, huh? You came out too quickly. Maybe you're too contemptuous of G-men, Gauerke. Maybe you couldn't resist having some fun with us. We'd better take your brain apart in hospital and see how much has decayed with age. There's another thing you were careless about.'

It was the smiling, confident Gauerke's turn to say, 'Yeah?'

'How could you know that your daughter had been abducted if you were supposed to be unconscious at the time? You slipped up then, in saying that, didn't you?'

'Did I?' It didn't wipe off that smile. Cheyenne was beginning to think that nothing would wipe it away, and then suddenly it dissolved and before him was a fat, arrogant face devoid of humour.

'I've had enough of this. I won't be questioned like a common crook. Who do you think you are? I'm Norm Gauerke, see? And I'm not going to submit to this cross-examination. I'm going to send for my lawyers . . . all of them. Meantime, get outa my house and stay out, blast you. And if you don't find my daughter, by God I'll bust you!'

Cheyenne stood his ground. 'That talk'll get you nowhere, Gauerke. I'm arresting you. Your first stop's the hospital, though I guess they won't find anything wrong with your skull. I reckon Russ must have rehearsed that blow, to be able to scratch your skin without hurting you. Get him out to a car, you men.'

They took him, shouting for his lawyers. He hadn't smiled for several minutes now.

Cheyenne walked out with October to a car. 'He's a cool devil,' he murmured. 'Arrogant . . . thinks because of his wealth and the reputation he's built up he can get away with anything . . . even murder.'

Paul Zaharias, by his side, shook his head doubtfully. 'You're going to have trouble in making this case stick, inspector. It'll be your word against his in court . . . you and Miss Raine here. Apart from what you two say, there'll be no other evidence against him. Well, the lawyers his money can buy will soon get around your evidence and discredit it.'

'You mean he'll be able to get away with it?' October was astounded. 'Why, it's incredible; it doesn't seem possible!'

Zaharias said slowly, 'That's the way it is. Knowing who's done a crime isn't the same as getting a court to agree with you. Courts are the criminal's best friend, so we say in the F.B.I.'

'That's being cynical.' Cheyenne was recovering his spirits. He smiled. 'You've got to prove beyond a shadow of doubt that a fellar's done something wrong before you get a conviction. And it's only right it should be that way. Better to let a few guilty people get away with their crimes than have innocent people suffer for something they've never done.'

October breathed, 'Boy, are you getting solemn!'

'That's because I'm obsessed with a solemn thought, right now.'

'And that is?'

'We'll never make that charge stick on Gauerke. I can see that right now.'

5

Charlie takes a vacation

They got into the car. Ahead of them, Gauerke had been lifted, chair and all, into the back of a squad truck. He was shrilly indignant, and for a philanthropist was using a lot of bad language.

Zaharias spoke as they turned down the long drive. 'I think there's something important you've overlooked, inspector. Mighty important.'

Cheyenne heard the concern in the younger man's voice and turned. 'Yeah?'

'You're going ahead with this charge against Gauerke?' Cheyenne nodded. 'Even though you think now you'll never be able to make it stick?' Cheyenne nodded again. 'Then this case'll bust you, inspector.'

Cheyenne looked ahead, considering that remark. After a moment he said, almost lightly, 'I hadn't thought of that, bub . . . sure, I guess you're right.'

He felt October's concerned gaze upon him.

'Then why don't you drop it . . . this case, I mean?'

'Drop the charges against Gauerke just because he can buy the best legal twisters in the profession?' The thought seemed to shock the big detective. 'What the heck, you can't do a thing like that.

'Not even for that.' Cheyenne's voice was grim. 'This would be a damn' fine country if the police and F.B.I. weren't prepared to take risks sometime. Now I know Gauerke's a crook, and I'm going to charge him with it. If he gets away with it . . . well, there's bound to be some mud sticking to him, and I suppose that's something.'

'A fat lot of good that'll do you if the big shots lever you out of your job for bringing a false charge against a highly respected citizen of the United States,' said October bitterly.

She knew how much Cheyenne loved his job, how proud he was to have risen from an Indian reservation to an inspector's office in the F.B.I. 'It'd break your heart, if you got thrown out.'

Cheyenne's brown, fight-scarred face turned towards her.

There was a smile on his face. She wondered why it was that when a man smiled you never noticed such things as broken noses, over-thick ears, and eyebrows bushed up by too-frequent contact with hard knuckles.

'Honey, who says I'm goin' to be thrown out, anyway? Who says we're gonna be licked by this dollar machine in a wheelchair?'

There was a note in his voice that thrilled her. She had heard it before. Cheyenne Charlie was in a fighting mood, he was beginning to fight back and he didn't give a hang about the consequences.

'What's in your mind, Charlie?'

'We're goin' to work fast. We're goin' to pin this on Gauerke . . . or my name's not Cheyenne Charlie.'

'It's Charlie Chey,' murmured October, but they weren't splitting hairs right then.

The Chicago HQ almost blew up when the squad arrived back with their prisoner. Within half an hour there was a big meeting at high level, and Cheyenne was detailed off to attend it. October was made to come along with her evidence, too, but being a minor employee of the Bureau she was sent outside when she had made her say.

All the highest police and F.B.I. officers of Chicago were there, and they looked mighty concerned. The commissioner said, 'This story's so incredible I can hardly believe it. It's the first breath of suspicion that we've ever heard directed against Norm Gauerke.'

'And you don't believe me, do you?' asked Cheyenne softly.

The commissioner said, 'I think you might have misunderstood a lot of things, inspector. I'm not saying that in any carping spirit, but you know how fallible the mind is as a witness. Also, you must remember that you had been through a very rough time immediately before meeting Gauerke. You can't lose blood as you did and not suffer in some way afterwards.'

'Meaning I suffered a few delusions where Gauerke was concerned?'

The commissioner was a very straight, honest man. He said, 'I don't know what to think, Chey, and please don't get it into your head that I'm saying anything against you. We don't know you here in Chicago except by repute, but you have a fine record. I'm quite sure you believe exactly what you are telling us.'

'But your opinion is that I am making a mistake . . . one mighty big mistake?'

The commissioner shrugged. He looked round at the other serious faces. 'I think we all feel you might have done. After all, Chey, if crooks did harbour themselves on Gauerke, they could make him do anything they wanted him to do simply by threatening his daughter, just as he said. There's no law we can lay against a man in that predicament. And they did run off with the daughter, according to your own evidence.'

'She went off with them . . . and so did the doc,' corrected Cheyenne. 'But my impression was that that getaway was something previously planned and rehearsed just in case something did go wrong. It was a bit of play-acting designed to provide the cunning Gauerke with an alibi.'

'Yes, yes, perhaps you're right.' The commissioner didn't look at Cheyenne now. 'I must say, though, that it seems far-fetched, relating as it does to Norm Gauerke.'

Cheyenne sighed. 'Norm Gauerke. Around here people breathe his name as if he was one of the ten angels. Look, I'm a stranger to Illinois . . . we've got our own millionaires back in California. Plenty of 'em. Maybe if you told me something about Gauerke I'd understand why you're . . . scared of him.'

'Scared?' Every head came up in indignation. Cheyenne was unmoved.

'That's how it seems to me.'

The commissioner seemed to swallow, then spoke quietly. 'Norm Gauerke is one of the best-liked men in Illinois. Whenever money is needed, he puts his hand into his pocket — deep.'

'I've been told something about that. But go back a bit further. How did he make his millions?'

'Railroads. He built railroads from the

stockyards out to the cattle countries. I guess he owns thousands of miles of track, and they bring him a few million a year out of charges.'

'Railroads?' Cheyenne was interested. 'I know something about railroading. You chiselled people out of their land, or hired huskies and drove them off. Then you laid your track and because it was the only one to that part of the country, you held it to ransom. The country, I mean. A lot of millionaires today got their money that way. I guess they were exciting days.'

He stopped abruptly, thinking. Then he let the thought lie fallow at the back of his brain and concentrated on what the inspector was saying.

'We have to be so careful in making charges against a person a big as Norm Gauerke. Why, after the things he's done for Chicago, you'd have people up in arms against you if you insulted him — and charging Norm Gauerke would be a darned big insult to him, of course.

'He's becoming more than a local figure, too. Look at this park he's opened for celebrities out at Lake Shore. Where you were, Chey.' Cheyenne nodded. 'He's out to put America ahead in the way of artistic genius, and he's doing it by bringing the best brains of the country together in the hope that they will stimulate each other to better work. He'll be a national figure himself, the rate he's going on. He'll run for senate soon, you can bet. Okay, with a man like that how can we accuse him of being leader of a gang of hoodlums?'

Cheyenne rose. 'I see what you mean. You think we'd never make the charge stick.'

'That's a certainty.' — Grimly. 'The word of a man and a girl, both strangers to Chicago, against Illinois' proudest citizens. Find your own answer to that, inspector.'

Cheyenne sighed, but there was glinting good humour in his brown, Indian eyes.

'Very well. That means you won't press with any charges?'

The commissioner looked round at his companions. They gave the briefest of nods, each in turn. 'That's what it amounts to, Chey. Sorry, you know, but — ' He shrugged. Cheyenne knew he wasn't a bit sorry.

He said, 'I'll be going back to duty, then.'

There was something in the way he said it that brought suspicion to the commissioner's eyes. He called, 'Oh, inspector.'

Cheyenne stopped and turned.

The commissioner spoke softly. 'I know your reputation, inspector. You're known as the Man Tracker in the service, the man who never lets a wrongdoer get away. Right?'

Stonily Cheyenne said, 'It might be.'

He saw the commissioner clasp his hands and clench the fingers quickly. 'My guess is you're going to walk out of this door determined to lay Gauerke by the heels. By hook or by crook you're out to get him now, aren't you?'

The other men there stirred indignantly at the suggestion, but the indignation was directed against Cheyenne.

The special operator looked the commissioner straight in the eye 'That's about it. Except for one thing. There's no need for hookin' and crookin' where Gauerke's concerned. The crookery's all on his side. I get my men, but I get 'em fair. I don't frame or fix my charges. I don't need to.'

'Inspector, I'm giving you warning.' He looked into a stern face eyes steely under bushy white eyebrows. 'I think that blow on your head did you no good. I think you've developed a complex about Gauerke. I'm warning you, if you do anything vindictive or reckless, you'll get no protection from this office. You'll be on your own, understand?'

Cheyenne nodded. 'I understand.'

Down below October was waiting for him. She looked cool and smart in her summer outfit, far different from the flashy moll of an hour or so ago. But her hair was still that painful dyed yellow.

Cheyenne looked at it and said, 'Honey, I don't like corn-yaller hair, though it's the fashion in Minnesota among the squareheads. Me, I like you as you were before.'

October demanded, 'Tell me what happened.'

He was still looking at her hair. 'It used to be such a nice blonde, and there was that dark streak in it that made it look different.'

'Leave my hair alone, darn you. I yallered it for you, you big lug, didn't I? I want to know what happened, so quit trying to talk me round the corner.'

Cheyenne gave in. Sighed, 'It's not good news, honey. They're not going after Norm Gauerke.'

'Just because he's a millionaire?' October was indignant again. That day she had been indignant quite a lot.

'No.' Cheyenne was fair to his superiors. 'I don't think a man's millions influence that bunch.' He sighed. 'Well, the fact is they can't believe anything against this public benefactor, and they're inclined to think that blow on the head dizzied me up more than something. They didn't say it, but you could see it on their faces. They think I'm a bit screwy.'

'I see.' October tapped the rubber flooring with an extended toe. She was as disappointed as the G-man. 'So what now?'

'Why, I'm going after him, that's what.

Knowing him for what he is, do you think I'd let him have the laugh on me?'

'Okay. But say 'We're going after him'. I'm with you, brother, don't forget.'

Cheyenne looked into that resolute oval of a face, into eyes that were blue and determined, and laughed. 'You're sure some fire-eater,' he exclaimed, then hugged her arm in his. 'Okay, we're in this together. We're going out to get the biggest man in Chicago, and this time we'll see that the charges stick.'

'And if they don't?'

Cheyenne sighed. 'I guess I'll be out of the service, then.'

They walked along. October thought that bit out and came back with a bright thought. 'Why, that wouldn't be too bad at that. Then you could marry me and we'd live happily ever after. Or am I being un-maidenly again?'

Cheyenne's chin stuck out. 'Un-maidenly or not, if I don't get Gauerke, darn it, I'll marry you and raise chickens.'

'You flatter a girl so.' October sighed. 'But — I know how it is. The service before everything.' That's what Cheyenne always said. He was married to the F.B.I. and didn't intend to commit bigamy.

Her heart felt just a bit heavy. She loved this big lug, but that didn't seem to get her anywhere. He just wasn't the marrying kind . . .

Cheyenne grinned, 'Let's go into the nearest place that sells a slap up meal. Chicken, I could go for. Plenty of it.'

October recovered her spirits and said, 'Let's go. Chicken it is. The prisoner ate a hearty breakfast — that's something like, isn't it?'

Cheyenne thought of the powerful Norm Gauerke and decided maybe it was something like.

* * *

Norm Gauerke went home from the hospital in his own big, specially constructed car. Within an hour suits were filed against the State of Illinois, the commissioners of police, the Federal Bureau of Investigation — and Inspector Chey. Norm Gauerke's lawyers were out to earn their fees.

And next day, sure enough, Gauerke got through to the police and reported that he had received a typewritten demand for a hundred grand in return for his daughter. The note also said that for a further ten thousand dollars they would release Gauerke's personal physician, Dr. Henry Coltnus. A doctor never does rate as high as a millionaire's daughter.

Cheyenne snorted when he heard about the ransom note. 'It's all part of the alibi he's fixin' for himself. Maybe he'll even hand over the dough, just so's to make things look good. Now, I wonder where the gang can have hid up . . . and the girl and the doc?'

He wasn't allowed to go out and see Gauerke, when the Bureau officially moved in on the kidnapping. Joe Hencke broke the news to him. Big Joe didn't like doing it, either.

'You're not on this case, Charlie,' he told him. 'Now, it's no good you arguing with me; I've got my orders You came here after Red Heydendahl. Okay, you fixed Red. Now you go back to California and tell 'em Chicago's still steeped in crime.'

Cheyenne blew up for a minute. 'Hell, they can't do this to me. Of course I'm on this case. Didn't I spring it open by getting taken for a ride in the first place? Okay, so what if I do come from Los Angeles office; I can work here till this thing's settled.'

Hencke said, 'You can't. That's just it. Maybe they think it would be undiplomatic for you to go on this Dilys Gauerke kidnapping case. After what you said about him . . . well I guess things wouldn't pan out.'

Cheyenne rose. 'Looks like Gauerke runs the Bureau around here,' he said shortly, and went out.

He was sore, and even October couldn't console him for a while.

He found her in the canteen, sipping coffee on a high stool. 'You're all burned up,' she told him, after one swift glance at that brown, set face.

He nodded to the attendant for a coffee. 'Wouldn't you be after being politely told to mind my own business and go home?'

'They've done that to you?' He nodded

and reached for his coffee as it came up. 'What are you going to do about it?'

He told her. 'I'm going to take a vacation to match yours. Let's go send a telegram to the L.A. office and tell 'em what I intend to do. Reckon a bullet in the head's a good reason for a coupla weeks off.'

And then he went to find that bright, nice young G-man called Paul Zaharias. He even took Paul out with them that night, just so that he could keep him talking. October protested that that was overdoing it. She'd come all this way to meet him and he couldn't find time to take her out alone for one evening! She sulked. It didn't worry Cheyenne any.

Paul told him a lot that was interesting about the Chicago underworld. 'It's not like it was in the Capone era, but it still takes millions out of the pockets of Chicago taxpayers, one way or another. Maybe you've heard of some of the gangs, operating semi-legally?'

Cheyenne said, 'Sure. Hanky Hahn and his flower racket. Suverkrup and Barce.

They're the three big mobs nowadays, they tell me.'

'Yeah. They're smart. They employ slick lawyers to keep 'em apparently within the law. But we know they're runnin' crooked, and we're waitin' for a slip.'

'Waiting can be a long game.'

October broke in, 'Shouldn't I know it? Six months without a letter from Charlie; then when we meet he brings a boy friend out for supper. I spy Joe Hencke. I'm going to share his table. He loves me a lot by now, so he tells me.'

Cheyenne went on talking. October repeated, louder, 'I said, he tells me quite a lot now. Says I'm a smart girl.'

The Fed turned his brown Indian eyes upon her. 'I heard you first time. So what? So long as he pays your bill, why should I worry?' She was moving away; she didn't see the grin on that bronzed pan. 'Hey, October.'

She turned.

He said, softly, 'But if I catch him holding your hand, I'll break his neck . . . and yours, too.' Then he turned back to the astonished young G-man.

October gulped. 'That's passion,' she told an inoffensive man at the next table, and walked across to the Chicago Fed's table.

He told her, 'Sweetheart, you're welcome. I came here to celebrate. I got a certain editor in a corner this evening, and the things I said to him. So I came here, feeling good. Now I'm feeling better.'

'So much as touch my lily white hand,' October warned, 'and my soul mate promised to crack your neck for you.'

'You know, he's a nice guy, that fellow,' said Hencke admiringly. But all the same he didn't linger long on the handshake. Maybe he wasn't too well acquainted with Indian blood.

When Cheyenne collected her to take her to her hotel, she could see he was pleased about something. He'd also got his plans fixed, that she also could see.

'What's cooking?' she demanded. 'And why are you so pleased?'

He helped her into a cab, gave the address. 'Something I just heard. Zaharias says war's broken out among the Chicago gangs. They haven't had a good war for years, and everyone's standing on the sidelines and hoping to hell they'll exterminate each other.'

'But why should that please you suddenly?'

'Well, the funny thing is that Barce, Suverkrup and Hahn aren't doing anything to each other, though they're the only gangs of importance in Chi today. The war's being forced upon them . . . by another mob, a mob seemingly new to these parts. Barce, Suverkrup and Hahn are bitter about it. They claim it isn't legal; they were in first.'

'A new mob? You think . . . '

'I think it could be Russ Amann and playmates. And the way I see things now, that puts Norm Gauerke as gang-leader starting a war against established gangs here in Chicago.'

October snuggled back into the cushions as the cab driver risked his life in a race to beat the lights at each intersection.

'Cheyenne,' she told him frankly, 'I'm puzzled. A lot of things don't fit. Here's

Gauerke spending millions on charitable enterprises, and then it seems that he is playing gangsters on the quiet.' She sat up. 'You don't think this is another of his ideas . . . that he's opening up a war on crime in Chicago, because the police are pretty helpless? Could it be that he's setting crooks to catch crooks, and he's really on the level?'

Cheyenne considered that angle carefully. 'Meaning that he's a good guy burning to give Chicago the justice its tape-bound police can't provide for it?' He shook his head. 'There's one thing makes that inconsistent.'

The cab driver risked his life for the last time and screamed to a halt outside October's hotel. When he was paid off . . . he seemed satisfied to go on risking his life for a dollar tip . . . October said, 'What was that thing?'

'His eyes.' Cheyenne halted outside the big doors. 'No guy who can keep laughter in his eyes while he discusses murder can be a genuine philanthropist. Well, honey, I'm going back to snatch some sleep. I'll pick you up around noon.'

'Where are we going?'

'I think we'll meet Hanky Hahn, who sells flowers in a big way.' He was about to turn when an idea appeared to strike him. 'Oh, yes. About tomorrow. You'll take those clothes off.'

October's eyes shot wide open.

' . . . wear those moll's clothes again, will you? You'll be Red Heydendahl's moll again tomorrow.'

October gasped. 'Red Heydendahl? But . . . '

Cheyenne shrugged. 'It should be safe enough. Paul thinks that Hanky Hahn's mob are all local boys. They wouldn't know Red if they saw him. It's a risk, maybe, but if I'm to nail friend Gauerke I guess I'll have to take some risks.'

This time he was going. She called him back. 'But why go to Hanky Hahn?'

'There's a saying, if you want to know about a fellar don't ask his friends . . . go to his enemies. I reckon Hahn will be that if he knows who's upsetting his flower cart.'

And this time he went. He was down three steps when he heard October wail,

'Oh, Charlie. Just leaving a girl flat like that.'

'Shucks!' He snapped his fingers. 'The things I forget.' He came back and took her in his arms. She closed her eyes. This was worth travelling all the way from New York for.

When he released her he said, confidentially, 'You know, I don't know why I don't do that more often. It's not bad at that.'

And then he went. October got the air back into her frame, eased against the bruises of her ribs and went inside. She was thinking: Man, can he kiss a girl! Maybe once in a while with Charlie is quite enough.

6

Hanky Hahn

Cheyenne dropped in at the office next day before collecting October from her hotel. Joe Hencke grinned, 'You should look after that girl. Me, I'd take October any day and leave the worms to get Zaharias.'

Paul didn't say anything. He was looking at Cheyenne and his eyes were knowing. Cheyenne hadn't told him his plan . . . that might have strained loyalty at some time, possibly . . . but he was shrewd enough to know that the L.A. man wasn't staying on in Chicago for a vacation, as he had declared.

Cheyenne said, casually, 'Paul was telling me last night that you went up to see Gauerke yesterday. How was the old . . . er, philanthropist?'

'He was exactly as you'd expect a father to be with a kidnapped daughter.'

'Huh, huh.' Cheyenne politely did not express his doubts. Unexpectedly Paul Zaharias supported him.

'Joe, I was there with Cheyenne when Gauerke . . . er, came to consciousness. I know Gauerke and his reputation, but all the same I can tell you this . . . that was a phony recovery, and Gauerke didn't bother, just at that moment, who knew it.

He was in a cussed mood, I guess and didn't give a damn who was around. I got the impression that something had riled him . . . '

'Something?' Cheyenne grinned. 'That's a plain understatement. To be suddenly surprised in your best drawin' room, and get caught with a parcel of hoods, well, that is riling.'

'Sure. Well, Gauerke looked to me like a man indulging in bravado . . . reckless, just trying to show he could keep his end up. We've talked about it since, all the boys who were up there, and that's how we all feel about the so-and-so.'

Something warm went racing through Cheyenne's veins. He sighed. 'Why didn't you tell me this last night, Paul? I was beginning to think I was on my own, that the Bureau was solid against me.'

Paul grinned. 'You were so darned busy asking me questions about other things, I never got around to it. And then you got to watching that Joe Hencke here didn't start to hold your girl's hand, and I never did believe in talking shop with a jealous man.'

Hencke said, 'This embarrasses me. I know what the other man feels like when he meets the outraged lover.'

The outraged lover grinned. He could take a lot of kidding from these fellows.

Then Hencke got serious. 'I'm going to tell you something, Charlie. You thought the big chiefs were dead against you, yesterday. But, you know what? Right after you left 'em, down came a call to me. And you know what that call was? You're on the Gauerke case. Go to it . . . and work on the assumption that Inspector Chey is right . . . and Gauerke's a wrong 'un.'

'That's highly gratifying.' And Cheyenne had the warm feeling again inside him. This was why he loved his work with the Bureau. They never let a fellow down.

'Sure,' said Joe Hencke. 'But it's what I expected. An experienced man like you doesn't go spinnin' cobwebs that can be destroyed by a puff of sarcasm from a court judge. No, sir, they knew you had some substance to your story.'

'They'd a queer way of showing it.'

'That was to get you out of the way.' Hencke grinned. 'You've got a reputation for being unorthodox, Charlie, and they figured they couldn't take any risks with a bird as powerful as Railroad King Gauerke. Put it another way, maybe they just plain went and changed their minds after you'd gone, like ordinary people.'

'Whichever way it was, it will make my vacation all the sweeter.'

Paul said softly, 'Betcha you tote a gun on this vacation.'

Cheyenne looked at him. There was a grin back of his brown eyes. 'You betcha I do . . . in Chicago.'

So Paul said, 'Some vacation,' and his eyes expressed doubt about the last word. Hencke looked quickly at the special agent. But all he said was, 'Cheyenne, there's just one thing.'

Cheyenne turned at the door. There was something significant in his brother inspector's voice.

'Yeah?'

'I got a curious impression, talking to Gauerke. I decided he was bluffing about that letter for ransom, though he thought he was kidding me. I reckon millionaires don't make good actors. Yeah. But for all that I got an impression that he was a very uneasy man . . . and his unease had something to do with the kidnapping.'

Cheyenne said, 'That's interesting. Now, I wonder what it could be?'

Hencke shrugged. He hadn't any idea. So Cheyenne announced that he was off on his vacation, and went out. When he had gone, Paul and the inspector looked at each other and grinned. Then Paul said, 'Yeah, like hell he's staying in Chicago in high summer on a vacation.'

Even Cheyenne couldn't kid the F.B.I.

A sulky October was lurking in the hotel lounge when Cheyenne called for her. He looked with approval at the frizzed up yellow hair, the painted little face and the garish, boudoiry outfit. 'You sure look the part, sweetheart,' he said tactlessly. Or maybe he was kidding her, she never could tell.

October snapped, 'I feel like a tramp. I came down to meet you, and you couldn't hear the traffic for wolf howls. Even the kid on the elevator got fresh and asked me was I home evenings after eight?'

Cheyenne was feeling good. He suddenly laughed, took her in his arms, and kissed her. They were tender kisses, not like the usual bear hugs, and it surprised her. It put her in a good mood again.

They went across town to Hanky Hahn's office. It was a class block of offices where the Hahn gang operated from. They took the express to the eighteenth floor, then the slow elevator another three floors beyond. In the centre hall, as thronged as any main street with shoppers, with brilliantly lighted windows all around, they saw the offices of The Chicago Florists Mutual Benefit Association.

It operated, perhaps logically, from a big flower shop itself — 'Hahn's Florist', they could read as they approached.

Cheyenne had to hand it to Hanky. It sure was a swell store. The display was brilliant, and Hahn had gone to a great deal of trouble to get the lighting just so in order to make his wares stand out. It was quite easily the most attractive shop in that skyscraper assembly of attractive shops.

They went in. The girls who served were such exquisite creatures it made you feel humble to approach them. So Cheyenne picked on a demure young thing of around sixteen who looked less haughty than the other assistants. Young kids have a habit of opening up a bit more than older girls.

He smiled brilliantly, winningly. Said, 'I believe you sell flowers.' Though that wasn't exactly a scintillating start. The kid said, 'See them things in them vases?'

Cheyenne nodded.

'They ain't candy?'

Cheyenne said, 'No,' wishing he had picked something older, after all.

'Then I guess they're flowers.' The kid nodded calmly.

'Sure, mister, I guess we do sell flowers.'

Cheyenne said, 'A fresh dame.'

October put on her act and said, 'Gimme that dame for five minutes and I'd twist the freshness outa her.'

And the kid said, 'No, you wouldn't, Hardboiled. For why, because the union's getting stronger even than Hanky Hahn. Reckon we're getting mighty democratic, nowadays,' she said complacently.

Cheyenne thought, 'Looks like Hanky Hahn might be slipping in a few directions all at once.' But all he said was, 'Hanky Hahn. That's the guy. I came to see him from Detroit. Look, show me where to find him, sister.'

'You gotta have big business before you get in to see Hanky,' the kid said stonily, and her eyes implied she couldn't believe he was big in anything.

But in the end they got her to take them into a back region, where the high, wide windows looked out across the great lake. That was where they found Hanky Hahn, in an office as lovely as a millionaire's home.

A secretary took them from the pert kid. Cheyenne put on his wary, tight-lipped act. Said, 'I gotta see Hanky. No, he don't know me. But he'll want to see me. Tell him there's a fellar outside must see him about flowers . . . a lotta flowers . . . a lotta flowers. All the flowers in Detroit. Tell him they're there, just waiting for the pickin'.'

While the secretary was inside, October said in a small voice, 'Charlie . . . you're taking an almighty risk in coming here.'

'You scared?' That thought hadn't occurred to him before. She shook her head indignantly. 'You can go back to your hotel if you like.'

But October wasn't going. Where Cheyenne went, she was going. 'Put it down to my jealous nature,' she cracked. 'I'm not having you alone among these hothouse flowers.' But she wasn't looking at the flowers, she was looking at the exquisites who were drifting around with armfuls of blooms.

Cheyenne grinned. Then the secretary came back to say the boss would see them.

They went in. As the door closed behind them, a curious sensation seemed to develop in October's back. She had a feeling that that door closed the way out to a bigger, safer world . . . and it wasn't nice, to feel that they were in a trap, and they had walked there voluntarily.

The room was big and bright in delicate cream and leaf green; the sun filtered through slatted blinds that yet permitted a view of the panorama outside. And there were tall flowers in slender vases everywhere.

A big polished desk occupied the centre of the office; around the room were deep chairs and comfortable settees. There was a man sitting behind the desk, and other men seated against the walls.

That was the first thing that Cheyenne noticed. Those men were sitting so that anyone coming into the centre of the room must be under complete supervision all the time they were in the office.

They didn't look office warriors, either. They had a familiar flat, yellow hardness to their pans; they had eyes that were slatted; as men's eyes go when they have been bumped around a bit; and their clothes were the flashy clothes that you got in less exalted circles than a swank skyscraper office.

Cheyenne saw this, slowly crossing the thick pile carpet. Then he looked at the bub sitting behind the desk. Hanky Hahn himself.

He saw a man who might have been thirty and yet could have been nearly twice that age. A man with a long narrow face that made him look a thin man, and it was only when you looked closer that you saw he had beef under his clothes.

He was tall, though not quite as tall as Cheyenne; going spare on top. But it was his face that Cheyenne didn't like. It really was a thin face; it looked as though someone had squashed it, elongating every feature including the teeth, and yet leaving the chin receding.

Cheyenne looked at those long, nicotine brown teeth and that drooping, pendulous underlip that showed red gum beyond, and thought of a camel that had had its head stuck through a mangle.

Hanky Hahn was no beauty.

But Hanky Hahn didn't want to be a beauty. Hanky just wanted money. He was a simple soul. Most people want good looks, good health . . . and money. Hanky would get by with money only, though he wanted plenty of that.

Hahn grunted, 'I didn't get your name,' and made no pretence of a welcoming smile.

There were two chairs close to the big desk. Cheyenne shoved back his hat so that the plaster could be seen above his eyebrow, and dropped easily into the chair. October sat down, hitched up her dress, and went to work like mad on her chewing gum.

Cheyenne smiled thinly. 'I didn't give no name.'

Hahn's eyes flickered. 'Maybe you should start right now, then.'

Cheyenne looked deliberately round from face to face before replying. He didn't recognise anyone, and he guessed that none had been working in California in the time he had been there. It still didn't make it safe, but it gave him a chance. He nodded, as if satisfied about something.

'Okay. The name's . . . Heydendahl.

Red Heydendahl. This is my girl.'

That lip sagged so much at the information that it looked like a double chin.

'Heydendahl?'

'Yeah.' Cheyenne slipped into the role of tough guy on the run, playing risky chances. 'I'm trying to get outa Chi, see? The place is too hot. I thought you might like to help a guy.'

There was not a man seated now at those chairs and settees around the wall. They had risen and come forward silently over that yielding carpet and were staring as if fascinated at the G-man.

'Red Heydendahl?' exclaimed one skinny rube with the pinpoint pupils of a dope eater. 'Jeez, I'm meetin' Red Heydendahl himself, just fancy!'

Hahn snarled, 'Shaddup. I'll talk. How do we know this guy's Red? Do any of your know him?'

They were silent.

Hahn said, 'You got anything to say to that?'

Cheyenne shook his head. 'Not a thing . . . except I'll blast your guts out if you send for a cop.' His hand was on his chest, and he looked mean and capable of going for his gun. He thought he saw a flicker of approval in those close-set ferrety eyes.

Cheyenne said, ‘Look, I don’t know you either, but I gotta take chances. I lit outa Cal because the place got too hot for me. I arrived in Chi . . . and found the place still hotter.’

‘Why d’you come here?’

‘A friend of mine said for me to join him and his mob here in Chi. Only that friend was no friend of mine.’ He looked at October who was giving a nice imitation of a mouse-brained blonde. ‘My girl was once his dame. I took her off him. I thought he wouldn’t mind . . . ’

‘The hell,’ cracked October, ‘that’s a nice thing to say.’

Cheyenne said, toughly, ‘I said it. Now shut up, you yap voice.’ She sulked back into her chewing. Cheyenne said, coldly, ‘Seems he did mind. He wasn’t where he said he’d be to meet me . . . but the Feds were, blast ’em.’

‘Your story hangs.’ Hahn was still cold but thawing. ‘How’d you get away?’

'The hell, that was luck. There was a fellar sittin' in his car when the shootin' started. So what does he do? He gets the hell out of it. And me, I just climb in as he starts to move off. The Feds thought that was me lyin' on the pavement, instead of that man-tracker Charlie Chey. It gave me time to beat the guns.'

'And you've been hidin' ever since?'

'Sure. I went home with that fellar in his car. He gave me an invitation to stop over with him.' Hahn's eyes looked doubt. 'He had a gun in his neck when he gave it. Then I contacted Mouse-brain here. So . . . how about smugglin' me outa town? Me, I'd like to hit New York. I could go for New York, I guess.'

Hahn's men were draping the desk, listening. Cheyenne could see that his story had hit the right note all along the line. It ought to have done . . . he'd spent half the night working it out.

There was silence for a few minutes, then Hahn said, 'Okay, Red. Looks like your story rings with the boys, so . . . so you're in.' He leaned forward, his lip drooping so that those inch-long teeth could be seen in their stained entirety.

'But you're not leavin' Chi yet, brother.' He leered. 'I got work for you. I need guns . . . men like you, Red. I'll hide you, and when things settle I'll get you into New York. But for a while, you're stayin' here and workin' for me.'

Cheyenne opened his mouth as if to protest, but inwardly he was jubilant. So far his plan had succeeded.

Hahn said, 'Close your pan, brother. I'm the big shot around here. I didn't ask yon to come to my office, so . . . why gripe? You'll get good pay, don't worry.'

Cheyenne relaxed, grumbling, 'It's hot here. I'd like to hit the breeze outa this blasted burg.' Then he asked, 'What's the work, anyway?'

'Gunnin' for hijackers.' Hahn got out a cigarette and lit up. Everyone decided to follow suit, including October who'd just got behind a new mouth.

Hahn said, 'You won't know the set up here in Chi, Red. But nowadays it's a nice, quiet, law-abiding place, with everyone mindin' his own business. That is, it was until a few weeks back, when someone started to stir up trouble.'

'Gun trouble?' asked Cheyenne softly.

'Gun trouble,' agreed Hahn, and then Cheyenne knew that this nice quiet business he was talking about were . . . rackets.

'There's me and Lou Barce and Rube Suverkrup. We got a nice arrangement whereby we don't tread on each other's corns. Why,' said Hahn enthusiastically, 'we even got to visitin' each other one time. Trouble was, some of the boys couldn't hit it off, so we dropped bein' that friendly.'

'You never moved on to each other's rackets, huh?' Cheyenne prompted.

'You said it, brother. And things were nice and profitable for everyone . . . until this gang opened up against us all.'

'This . . . gang?' Cheyenne felt that he was getting somewhere . . . fast. But then he'd expected to get such news here.

'Sure. Lou Barce got some of his boys tidied up down the stockyards one day. Straight afterwards he got a polite, typewritten note to say for him to get to hell outa Chi or else. And the 'or else'?

He'd be gunned out and his rackets taken over. Lou wouldn't move, so the new mob went in to move him. He can't transport a truck of beef without an accident happening to his vehicle. He's got so many bust up trucks, he can't run his racket any more.'

And Cheyenne knew the racket: 'Use my trucks when you want anything moving; otherwise I'll drive your trucks off the road.' Barce specialised in moving beef. Refrigerator trucks damage very easily and are vulnerable. Now he was finding how vulnerable his own expensive vehicles were to injury, Cheyenne thought. A case of the biter bit.

'Suverkrup's goin' out fast. He owns the beer joints down town. There's one gets shot up every night, and now no one ever goes near a Suverkrup beer parlour unless he thinks to get a suicide bullet. Suverkrup'll sell out . . . at a song . . . to the new mob any time. Or give out.'

'And you?'

Hahn took out a handkerchief and mopped his wet underlip. 'I'm fightin' back. That's why I need you. The only thing is . . . you can't fight back if you don't know who you're fighting.'

Red said, 'Let's know more about your racket. I got an idea maybe I know who's behind this mob.'

Hahn was startled. 'How would you know, just come to Chi?'

'That's why.' Cheyenne was fitting things together. 'I was told there was a new mob forming to take over rackets here in Chi. I came to join 'em. Well, that part was true . . . about a new mob wantin' guns . . . but it seems someone didn't want me in it and tipped off the Feds about me.'

'You know this mob, then?'

'Some of 'em. Not all. Russ Amann's a big shot in it, but not the biggest. Then there's the Kadoc brothers . . . and others I'll remember later.'

Hahn said, 'You've told us enough, brother. Rube Kadoc was with Lou Barce . . . looks like a double-cross. And Russ Amann was Number One gunnie for me until he disappeared a coupla months ago. By jeez, when I get hold o' that fellar . . . '

Cheyenne said, softly, 'You should go for the big boy behind those punks, Hank. They're dime-a-dozen gunnies. But there is a big shot . . . a real big noise . . . back of 'em, and he's the guy to fold up.'

'You know him?' That camel face looked eager.

'I got an idea maybe I do.' Cheyenne let his voice fill with cold menace. 'Maybe it's the same guy was once this doll's paycheck. Maybe it's the same guy was wantin' to see me rubbed out. Maybe.' Cheyenne used his imagination just then, but he put it over convincingly.

'And you'd like to rub him out?' This was talk that Hahn could understand.

'Yeah. I'm willing to stay on in Chi if you'll help me get the two-timing snake.'

They grew so cordial at that that Hanky Hahn couldn't even get around to telling about his racket without everyone first having a drink. But Cheyenne got the lowdown on the racket all the same.

It was the old one. Florists were told, 'You buy all your requirements apart from flowers from our Association.' When they were persuaded into agreeing, Hahn's boys went round to the manufacturers and roped them into the Association also. The subscriptions were steep for florists but astronomical for the manufacturers of florist's supplies.

But they had to pay.

Or go out of business.

Cheyenne asked, 'How d'you make 'em pay?'

Hahn lifted his eyebrows. 'Now, that's easy. A fellar don't pay, we back a truck through his window. No, the driver he don't run away. Why should he? It was an accident could happen to any guy. Anyway, the florist'll be covered by insurance.'

'I don't get it.'

'Look, brother, insurance covers repairs to property. It don't cover loss of business while the shop's shut because a new front's goin' up. Do that once or twice and they find it cheaper to join the association.' He got enthusiastic. It was a fascinating sight, to see that sallow, drooping, camel face getting excited.

'And it's legal. That is, so far as they can pin it on anyone. The cops can't touch us. What can anyone say about a truck skidding into a window? It happens all the time. Usually a coupla times and a hint from one of the boys is enough. Though one time we had to back four trucks through a fellar's window before he reckoned obstinacy didn't show dividends.'

Cheyenne said, 'It's a swell idea,' and made a note mentally of what he had heard. 'How's this mob hurtin' you, then?'

'They've been out and bust up the factories makin' the florists' supplies. No supplies, no need for subscriptions. We can't do a thing till this mob are cleaned out. I tell you, Red, it's costin' me a whole lotta dollars, this business.' He sounded very grieved.

'So,' said Cheyenne, 'we must clean up this mob. How?'

They looked at each other, those gunmen rats, and never a thought came to any of them. So Cheyenne prompted patiently, 'First thing is to find where they operate from. You got any ideas?'

One time, he thought, they probably operated from the park along Lake Shore, but they wouldn't be using that any more. So they had to find their new hideout.

Hahn said, 'We looked for Russ when he left us, but he'd just lit out from his apartment and no one knew a thing about him. We thought maybe he'd got into private trouble and had gone under. One of the boys went round the morgues out of curiosity but he never saw him there. He must have gone and joined the new boss. What did you say his name was?' . . . casually.

'I didn't. He's for me, that guy. All I ask is you should find him.'

That was something Cheyenne couldn't do, say, 'The big shot's Norm Gauerke.' Because gunning for Gauerke would have been too big a job for a racketeer like Hanky Hahn and he'd have known it. All he wanted was for Hahn to put him on the trail of the mob. Coming here seemed to have been a long shot that was mighty near to coming off . . .

Hahn said, 'Okay. I don't care who croaks him so long as he goes out quick. What next, Red?'

'Find Russ?' He looked round the men.

There wasn't a glimmer of hope from the lot of them. Cheyenne tried to prompt their minds.

'Look, try'n think where Russ might be. Try'n think of anything Russ said which might give us a clue.'

They thought. He knew they were thinking because he could hear their brains creak. But it was depressing, the result. Just nothing.

Maybe it made the hophead feel he ought to say something even if it was useless. Cheyenne heard his croak, 'I never did see Russ much. I was workin' the other side of town more. But the last time he saw me he didn't seem to like me much.'

'Go on.' Cheyenne was interested.

The hophead shrugged. 'There ain't no more to go on. I was in a ritzy eatin' joint with a dame when in he came — with a guy. He didn't see me until I went over to give him the big hello. Then he didn't seem so pleased. Maybe he thought I wasn't class enough for that place.'

'Who was the other guy? What was he like?'

The hophead had to think back and took his time. Hahn got impatient, but that wasn't any use and they all had to wait for the dope to remember.

'He was big and thin and young. Got smoothed back black hair. Yeah, and a slick li'l moustache like a Limey actor.' He kept on thinking, then nodded his dope-head. 'Sure, that was him. A doctor,' and then he looked blank as if he didn't expect his information to amount to a row of beans.

Cheyenne said, 'A doctor?' His thoughts leapt to Henry Coltnus, Norm Gauerke's personal medical man. It was queer how all strings led back in the same direction. He said, 'Go on, Dopey, you're doin' fine. Tell me more about the doc.'

But the hophead hadn't anything else to tell, just that Russ had looked annoyed and briefly introduced his companion as his doctor.

'His doctor.' Hahn nearly spat. 'The hell, Russ Amann never had need for a doctor that a bottle couldn't do.'

Cheyenne was sitting back in his chair, thinking hard.

Through his mind was racing the thought, 'Doctor's . . . deaths . . . and nice big wreaths.' He had a feeling that that was going to get him somewhere. He looked into that evil camel face and said, 'Hank, I know that doc. His name's Henry Coltnus, and he's a pretty fashionable doctor to have. I know something else, too . . . that doctor is in cahoots with your hijacker friends.'

Hahn got to his feet, and he looked suddenly pretty big. 'Then what are we waitin' for? We'll go round and talk to that guy, I guess.'

'Go round where?'

Hahn said, 'Why, to his home, of course.' And then Cheyenne told him that Coltnus didn't live there any more, though he didn't say why. He stood up, too, the excitement of the chase gripping him. Outside he heard a newsboy shouting, but the significance was lost on him.

'Doctors, death and floral wreaths,' he said to Hahn.

'Meanin'?'

'He'll be known to your customers,

some of them. They'll know a doctor better than most people, see? Okay, get your boys out now askin' all the questions they can about Coltnus. Maybe he's got interests in some nice, quiet little sanatorium or a convalescent home that'd be just fine as a front for a gang hideout.'

Hahn said, 'I don't know how I lived before you came into my life, Red,' and he looked fondly at the G-man.

October gathered her things. 'For me, he's a guy that talks too much. Me, I'm goin' places . . . if none of you gentlemen mind.'

When she was at the door she turned. 'Don't break a blood vessel over me while I'm out, Red,' she said. Cheyenne stiffened. 'I'll be right back . . . Red.'

Cheyenne thought, 'What the hell, Red-ing me like that.' Then he looked up He caught her eye for one fraction of a second, but what he saw there disturbed him.

If October wasn't desperate about something, he was a dope himself.

He found himself wisecracking, 'Don't hurry, I won't die out on you.'

Then October went, but going through the door he heard her voice say unpleasantly, 'I wouldn't bet on that,' and he knew she was tipping him off about some danger.

She didn't come back.

When they went to look for her, they couldn't find her, either.

And looking at Hahn and his boys, Cheyenne saw they were as mystified as he was about her disappearance.

7

The Glass Bubble

One of the boys came back to say that October had been seen hurrying out through the display centre. Cheyenne looked at him and decided that the guy was speaking the truth . . . this wasn't any monkey business on the part of Hanky Hahn and gang. He was wondering why October had taken a powder, when Hahn's voice grated.

'Where's that dame of yours gone to, Red?'

Cheyenne shrugged helplessly. 'By jeez, I'd like to know myself.'

The way he said it must have been reassuring to the narrow-faced mobster. 'I thought for a minute maybe you was up to some tricks.' Then his eyes narrowed. 'Sure she ain't, Red? We was talkin' about movin' in against Russ Amann and his boss . . . and you said that dame had been the boss's girl one time. Okay, so maybe she don't like to think of her ex bein' moved in against. Okay, maybe by now she thinks her ex has got somep'n you haven't got. Maybe she's gone back to him . . . to warn him.'

Cheyenne dug out a growl of primitive jealousy. 'If she's run out on me I'll carve rings round her neck.'

He got up. 'I gotta get outa here. Maybe she's gonna tip off the big shot . . .'

Hahn said, 'Sure. Maybe it won't be safe for you here now. You're gonna come with me to my apartment until the boys dig up somep'n about your doctor pal.' He turned on the gang. 'Get out. Make the rounds and ask questions about the doc. Ask questions all the time, see? And come back here with the answers. I want to find where the doc might be hiding up right now.'

They all went down together. Cheyenne looked about for October as he went, but he saw nothing of her. They got into the big Pontiac and roared off, just Hanky Hahn and Cheyenne together. Then the lights went against them and they screamed to a sudden stop. Idly Cheyenne looked out of the window. A kid was screaming hot news and the papers were going fast.

A man without a suit coat, showing jazzy patterned suspenders on top of a Honolulu shirt, bought a paper and opened it. It opened with the front page just for a fraction turned towards the G-man and three-inch bold headlines shrieked, '*Red Heydendahl dead — Cheyennne Charlie did not die*.'

Cheyenne sank back blinking. He thought, 'The hell, this is a fine time to release such news to the press.' And then he remembered something October had told him. About Joe Hencke. Getting in some nice snarls at a smart editor. Joe must have told the guy the truth last night, and here it was, published by that hardboiled editor as a scoop.

Cheyenne shrugged. Hencke hadn't done anything wrong. There seemed no purpose in keeping up the deception any longer. After all, he thought, I'm here on vacation; things like that shouldn't be worrying me.

He wondered if that was why October had ducked out on him. Maybe it had suddenly dawned on her what Hencke had meant by 'takin' down the pants of a too smart headline boy'. Maybe that's why she had ducked out . . . to be around if anything broke, around where she could help him most.

She was one smart girl, October Raine. Someday, by jeez, he'd up and marry her . . .

That squashed camel face shoved past him. Hanky Hahn had a dime in his hand. He started yelling to the newsboy, but the kid had a couple of other customers by now and kept him waiting. Sweat broke out on Cheyenne's brow as it became a race between the lights and the boy serving his customers.

The lights won. Just. The kid was coming across to them when the lights changed and the car went hurtling suddenly forward. They didn't stop again until they were at Hahn's apartment, and by that time he had forgotten about the newspaper. Cheyenne hoped the boys would be too busy digging up information for them to stop and read the early edition. It was a pretty safe bet, he thought, and decided to take a chance on it.

News began to come in almost as soon as they arrived. It mostly came by phone. A lot of the florists knew Dr. Coltnus, and he seemed, for a young man, very well established.

At first, though, all trails seemed to lead to the same place . . . a private hospital out on Shore Drive. It wasn't a big place, but reports said it had tone. According to one of the mobsters, the scalpels were all gold-tipped and even the swabs had natty lace edging. Cheyenne thought that might be an exaggeration, but gathered that Coltnus was in the money with his share in the place.

But the reports also suggested that the mob wouldn't be using the place as a hideout. It was too small to hide patients and a mob, and there were plenty of patients there just now.

Half an hour later they really got on to Coltnus's track. One of the boys came up to the apartment, quite a bit excited.

‘I found me a florist who does special jobs for Coltnus. You know, big expensive stuff, with words in forget-me-nots like, ‘The world won’t be the same now George has gone. It won’t.’ Just occasionally they’re told to deliver them across to the Glass Bubble, where some patient of Coltnus has suddenly died.’

‘The Glass Bubble?’ Cheyenne’s interest quickened. ‘A night club?’

The bub shook his head. ‘It’s a place you go to after an operation at the Coltnus hospital, where you get strength to be able to look at the bill. It’s a floating convalescent home, a coupla miles off shore, north along the lakeside out of range of the polluted city atmosphere.’

Hahn said. ‘I never knew you knew so many words, Joe.’

And Joe said, modestly, ‘I picked ’em up off the advertisement for the place.’

Cheyenne was thinking of a motor-launch disappearing out into the lake, thinking that a good place to terminate that voyage might be the Glass Bubble.

‘This boat . . .’ he began.

The bub shook his head. ‘It ain’t no

boat, brother. Boats are for ordinary guys. The Glass Bubble's just what it sounds like. It's a big bubble of glass floating high out of the water. It rides on submerged pontoons, and it's designed so that storms and high waves don't affect it none at all. It's got a big promenade deck where everyone sits out in the sunshine and enjoys bad health. Remind me to have an ulcer when I get into real big dough.'

Cheyenne got the picture. 'That'd be a swell hideout for the gang. They'd look like any other patients convalescing.' He was wondering how to get this information back to the Bureau. It mightn't lead anywhere, but he had a hunch that it was as good a place as any to look for the mobsters and their 'victims'.

Hahn said, thinly, 'If you're thinkin' of casin' the joint, you got no idea, brother. You get taken up in a waterlevel elevator, and there ain't no other way of gettin' aboard. If you was a spider, maybe you could get up them raft supports, but you got six legs more'n I c'n see right now if you are.'

'Like that?' Cheyenne wanted to get aboard that Glass Bubble . . . with those headlines chasing up and down the streets, he wanted to get away from Hanky Hahn quick, anyway. It wouldn't be healthy if any of the boys tumbled to his deception.

Hanky got the idea. 'Maybe your florist chum could help us?'

The bub thought. 'Maybe. But I wouldn't know. He's doin' a job with orchids right now . . . said it had to go out with a casket, urgent.' He got enthusiastic. 'Boss, he says that casket's lead-lined, and it's got real gold handles, and the paddin's nylon. It must be nice to have a casket like that,' he ended wistfully.

Cheyenne snapped his fingers. 'I got an idea. Look, Hank, we're goin' out to that florist. We're gonna find the mortician, and I'm goin' aboard the Glass Bubble in that casket, get me? When I'm aboard I'll find some way of operatin' that elevator and bringin' you all aboard.'

The boss said, 'Hell, Red, there's a big risk attached to it.'

Joe said, admiringly, 'Jeez, does this boy

like to get into trouble!'

But Cheyenne knew there'd be no more trouble for him on that bubble than he'd get in this apartment if he hung around long enough. He wanted to get the hell out of the place . . . and he hoped October was doing something about it, too.

Hahn said, 'It's your funeral, Red. Let's go.'

As they went out into the corridor they heard the phone start to ring. Cheyenne stiffened. Then Hahn said, 'Aw, hell, let it ring. It'll be one of the boys. He won't have nothin' to tell.'

They went down together. Cheyenne wondered if he'd got out just in time, if in fact that last call was a warning from one of the boys.

He breathed a sigh of relief as they came out into the bright sunshine. He felt he could handle two of them, provided they didn't get the jump on him, and he didn't intend to let them do that.

They went north to a fashionable suburb along the lake. The florist was an intelligent man. He said yes to everything that Camel Face propounded. Then they went out to the mortician who was no less intelligent. He wasn't in the Association, but he knew all about Hanky Hahn.

He took them in to view the finished casket. Cheyenne felt the weight. It was very heavy. He said, 'Rip the lead out. Then they won't notice my weight much.'

The mortician looked mortified but went to work. He put air holes under the handles and along the bottom, then gave his opinion that a guy might live in that thing for a few hours, but the hell it was gonna be hot this weather. And he also pointed out something highly important.

Once inside, a fellar couldn't let himself out.

Hahn's long teeth gnawed at a cigarette. 'You hadn't thought of that, Red. What're you gonna do about it?'

Cheyenne said, 'The hell, one way or another I'm goin' aboard that bubble. The big shot can't play me around like he has done. I reckon I'll just sit up with a gun in my hand when the morgue attendant opens up the casket. I don't reckon to find much trouble there.'

They made arrangements for Hahn and his mob to cruise around in launches until he could signal that he had control of the elevator. Cheyenne said that would be after dark.

He didn't say that he had no intention of bringing them on to the bubble. No, sir. By evening the mob would for certain know that Red Heydendahl was dead and he was an impostor. Once aboard that bubble and he was on his own.

He got into the casket. The lid came on and light dimmed and faded as the screws were tightened. It was the worst experience of his life. Panic began to mount inside him. He wanted to struggle, to shout to be let out. It was the utter helplessness of his situation that got him.

And suddenly it was very hot inside that casket, stiflingly hot. Sweat broke out on his face, and the backs of his hands felt clammy. He thought, 'What's it gonna be like maybe in a few hours' time?'

Then he thought: What happens if Hanky Hahn gets to know I'm not Red Heydendahl while he still has me in this casket?

It wouldn't be nice for him. He had visions of that casket being shoved into deep water long before they reached the bubble.

Then his Indian stoic training came to his aid. He relaxed, let his mind go dull and blank. He willed himself into as near to sleep as possible under the circumstances. The less energy he used, the less unpleasant his prison would be.

He felt the casket being lifted and carried. Then he knew they were aboard the mortician's swank funeral chariot. More lifting, seemingly hours later, then a gentle movement. That would be from a launch, though curiously he couldn't hear or feel engines inside that soft padded casket.

He didn't remember any change after that which might have indicated being transferred to the elevator of the Glass Bubble. Time just went by. He might have been in that casket three or four hours . . . on the other hand, it could have been three or four days; he had no way of knowing.

Then suddenly his brain woke up. He

could hear noise now and light began to filter in through a widening crack as the lid eased off.

Someone was unscrewing the lid.

He had the gun in his hand across his chest. He waited. The lid came partly off a couple of inches, and a blinding light hit Cheyenne. Someone was humming, 'I ain't got no body,' and making a mess of the tune at that.

The lid bumped off.

Cheyenne tried to rise immediately and point his gun at the singer, then found to his horror that he couldn't move. Just for those seconds he seemed not to have power in his limbs, as a result of lying in one position all that time.

His staring eyes saw a man's lank hair, then his thin, pink face, and light-lashed pale blue eyes. The eyes shot open, startled. He saw that mouth drop open then exclaim, 'By cracky, they didn't send it empty. The hell, I got two stiffs now.'

Cheyenne said, 'Up, Charlie,' and desperation gave him strength. Somehow he shot up between the close, padded walls of the casket. The movement gave the thin pink attendant heart failure.

Cheyenne sat silently watching him, his automatic pointing steadily at the man's chest. He was calculating, wondering if this was a straight guy or a crook. He had a feeling that no guy with a face as weak as that could be a crook. Maybe the guy could be trusted to help him.

The pink guy said, 'Sufferin' snakes, what game are you playing?'

Cheyenne said, dryly, 'They got standin' room only down under, so I decided to come back for a few years more.' Confidentially, 'You don't catch me queuing for anything, brother.'

The pink man said, 'You're a wise guy,' and Cheyenne didn't know which way to take it.

He got out of the casket. They were in a white-walled place that stank of antiseptics. The laying out chamber. Here was a stainless steel-topped table alongside his own, and on it lay the stiff. He was bald and elderly and looked a mound of stomach under the carelessly draped white shroud that didn't quite cover either his skinny ankles or his head.

The attendant backed towards the door. Cheyenne said, 'I can beat you to it . . . with a bullet,' and the fellow stood still.

He asked, 'Who are you? Not another of them tough guys, huh? I said they wasn't our kind.'

'You're a snob,' said Cheyenne pleasantly. He decided that this guy was straight.

'You mentioned tough guys. I'm interested in tough guys. That's why I came back from the dead. My name's Chey . . . Inspector Chey of the F.B.I.'

The attendant gasped. 'I just read the papers. It's like you said, Cheyenne Charlie came back from the dead. But I didn't reckon to be on hand when you arrived back.'

Cheyenne grinned. This rube had a sense of humour. He felt they were going to get along.

He took out his shield and showed it. The guy was impressed. Maybe he had read a lot of G-man novels.

Cheyenne said grimly, 'If you're a wise guy you'll co-operate with the F.B.I. If you don't, it'll be too bad. I'm aboard the Glass Bubble because I'm lookin' for some mobsters. I think they're here.'

The pink guy said, 'I know they are. I said all the time they weren't our class . . . and don't you call me snob none. These guys ain't got no manners. I gotta clean the decks, spare time, an' they spit all over the place. The sooner they're run off the bubble the better.'

'You know Dr. Coltnus?'

'Sure I know him. He's the guy been kidnapped, ain't he? We get a lot of patients from his hospital.' Confidentially . . . 'I got me an idea that on the quiet that guy owns this place. Frank Kendry's supposed to be boss, but me I think he's a stooge. The way he gives the big smile when Coltnus comes aboard . . . '

Cheyenne said, 'Sure, sure.' He didn't want this guy to go on talking forever. 'Coltnus isn't aboard right now?'

'Nope. How could he be when the papers say he's kidnapped?'

Cheyenne thought: Of course. Coltnus wouldn't dare show his face aboard his own boat while there was this pretence that he had been kidnapped.

He said, slowly, 'I gotta hunch he's aboard, all the same. That's where you come in, brother. You're gonna help the F.B.I. locate him.'

The pink attendant with the pale eyes seemed none too sure about helping anyone. Maybe he figured there was a lot of lead connected with the G-man stories he had read, and he didn't want to get in the way of a lump himself.

But with a man like Cheyenne Charlie it wasn't easy to hold out. Inspector Chey, F.B.I. special agent, had a way of appearing very tough at times.

When the attendant was finally in a co-operative mood, Cheyenne got the lowdown about the Glass Bubble. The big raft floated twenty feet above the water on top of steel girders connected with barely submerged pontoons. The first floor contained the private rooms of the convalescing patients, as well as offices, remedial baths, physiotherapy rooms, etc. On top was a great promenade deck that covered the entire area of the bubble. This was laid out with lawns and flowerbeds.

And above all was the gigantic glass dome from which it derived the name of the Glass Bubble.

Cheyenne said, 'You got a phone?' The attendant shook his head. 'Radio?' He nodded. 'What's the radioman like?'

The attendant wouldn't give an outright opinion. The fellar took too much ready money; maybe he was in strong with whatever was happening aboard the bubble. Cheyenne decided to leave radioing to an emergency.

He asked. 'If I go out about the bubble will my appearance cause surprise?'

'Nope, I guess not. We got plenty strange lookin' birds aboard right now.'

Cheyenne gulped a little and said, 'Thanks.' Then he went out, leaving a doubting attendant scratching his head alongside a corpse.

Cheyenne saw the elevator almost opposite. He was in a carpeted corridor that went straight the full width of the bubble. There were doors on either side, most of them with frosted glass windows set in. Cheyenne hardly needed to look to know that they led to the offices and physiotherapy wards. Around the first bend, however, there was a change. Here the floor was more richly carpeted; the place was softly lit, so that it looked like a corridor in a swank apartment block. There was no glass in these doors. When he peeped inside one room he saw that it was the richly appointed suite of one of the patient guests.

He saw an elderly woman walking slowly on the arm of a nurse far down the corridor, but otherwise the place seemed deserted. He looked at his watch. It was eight. He thought perhaps everyone was in the dining room having dinner, and that made him remember it was a long time since he had last eaten.

He could smell food down the corridor, but resisted it and climbed a broad stairway with potted palms on every little landing. He found himself on deck.

It wasn't dark yet, but lights were on everywhere, and the Glass Bubble looked warm and bright and inviting under the brilliant electrics.

He walked across floodlit lawns, and the heady smell of night-scented shrubs and flowers came drifting to his nostrils. It was nearly as nice as the odour of sizzling pork that he'd smelled below deck.

Few people were around, and even they were drifting towards another stairway across from him.

He walked to the side of the raft and looked out on to the broad Michigan. Strings of lights were going on all along the shore, a couple of miles away. It looked pretty; you didn't connect it with vice and gangs and danger.

Then he saw a small launch tearing in from the city harbour, then saw another . . . and focused on that.

This second was a big launch, and it was doing nothing in particular. That was why it aroused his suspicions. As it cruised slowly parallel to the shore half a mile from the raft, Cheyenne had the momentary impression of a shark on the prowl.

And he got the idea that maybe he was the prey.

That launch was big, big enough to take a couple of dozen gunnies. 'Could be it's Hanky Hahn and playmates,' he thought. But he wasn't going to signal them to come in. No, sir, if they didn't know by now that Red Heydendahl was dead, he was a squarehead.

And he wasn't. Indians have long heads.

He grinned. They were waiting, thinking he was going to let them get aboard the bubble. And when they were aboard they'd turn on him and shoot the daylights out of him? A nice little set up. Only, by sheer good fortune he'd spotted those headlines ahead of the Hahn mob.

He went down towards the busy dining room. There was the usual hubbub of an orchestra trying to be heard above the eating; waiters running around like obsequious penguins; and fat men and women frowning and worrying over the next course they had to order.

He paused on a landing and looked as far as he could across the big room. His eyes widened, then narrowed as he saw Russ Amann and two of the boys at a table over to one side.

So the mob was here.

He sighed with relief. Up till now he had backed one hunch after another, and all might have been wrong. But by good fortune the slender chain had held — and now he'd found the end of it, and it was as he had hoped and expected. Russ Armann and boys were hiding out on the Glass Bubble. He was willing to bet that the 'kidnapped' pair were along one of the corridors, enjoying a private meal in, say, Coltnus's office.

Cheyenne decided to eat and figure out his next move while doing so. Clearly he must get in touch with the shore and bring the F.B.I. on the scene. But — how could he do that with this mob in control of the bubble, and an equally hostile mob prowling between him and the shore?

Calmly, the special agent took a seat at an empty table that was close by the stairway. A waiter saw him, hesitated then came hurrying up. Cheyenne looked him straight in the eye and gave his order from the menu. The waiter suddenly smiled, snapped his fingers and said, 'Number 43?'

Cheyenne said, 'Yeah, Number 43.'

And that seemed to please the waiter no end and he went off quite happily and brought Cheyenne his first course.

Cheyenne disappeared before reaching sweets and desert.

He wanted to get back to the morgue before the corridor became too crowded, and he slipped off ahead of the other diners. That morgue and the not unfriendly attendant seemed the safest place aboard ship for him. He also had ideas in getting the attendant to lead him to the radio operator so that a call might be put in to the shore. A gun often makes a radio op do things he has been paid not to do. He could do that now, knowing that the raft was harbouring criminals.

He was fifty yards down that last corridor where the offices were, when he heard the distant whine of the elevator. Suddenly he remembered that small launch careering straight for the bubble. He thought: Jeez, maybe someone's coming aboard.

For a moment he thought maybe Hanky Hahn might have taken advantage of the moment and forced his way into the elevator, too, but when he looked out through one of the round portholes he could see that long launch still prowling half a mile out. Maybe hadn't been in near enough to seize their chance.

Cheyenne hesitated, then stepped through some swing doors. Inside was in darkness, but he got the smell of steamy water and thought he could be in the Turkish or Russian baths.

He waited in the darkness. A gate clanged along the corridor, then he heard soft movements along the carpeted floor.

He was watching through a crack between the doors.

Something familiar came within view. A wheel. Someone pushing. A wheelchair.

And big, bald, toothy Norm Gauerke was sitting bolt upright in the chair.

Only he wasn't grinning. There was murder in his eyes.

8

Double-cross

Cheyenne waited until they had passed, then carefully looked out after them. He was in time to see them stop outside a door; Gauerke said something to his attendant, and the man went off round the end of the corridor — it could be to keep watch, Cheyenne thought. Gauerke wheeled himself through the door.

Cheyenne stepped out into the corridor. At any moment he expected the place to flood up with guests returning from their dinner, and with them would be the mobsters.

He hesitated, uncertain what to do. He felt that it was most urgent now to get that radioman co-operating. If Gauerke could be found in cahoots with the gang it would bust completely his story of a kidnapping.

But Cheyenne hesitated because he had

a natural desire to know what Gauerke was saying and doing right now. There was a puzzling element that baffled the G-man, and he badly wanted the answer to it.

Why was multi-millionaire Norm Gauerke acting as gang leader in a war against the Chicago underworld?

He crossed to an observation bay and looked out into the near-night. Chicago was a distant cluster of merry, twinkling lights. Closer, creeping along the black water he could see a north-bound freighter just pulling out, and way back a lake steamer was returning home in a blaze of deck lighting . . . Cheyenne even heard the distant strains of its dance orchestra.

But that long low launch was still prowling way out there. Cheyenne grinned. 'I'll bet Hank Hahn's as mad as hell,' he thought. Hank Hahn badly wanted to get to grips with the mob that had begun to run him out of business . . . and he'd also very much want to meet up with the man who had kidded him he was Red Heydendahl.

At which moment something squat and black seemed to flit away from the Glass

Bubble. Cheyenne got a glimpse of the vessel and groaned.

It was a city fire float on patrol. If only he could have been on deck and signalled to her!

But now she was going away fast; he'd lost his opportunity.

He sighed . . . then stiffened. Faintly he heard the sound of a shot . . . then more shots. A girl started to scream, then abruptly shut up. Still no one showed along the corridor.

Cheyenne padded down to that door through which Gauerke had disappeared. He was almost there when it was shoved open. The G-man stepped into a doorway and watched.

Henry Coltnus came out. Only, he didn't walk out. He crawled through the open doorway . . . came out like a weary, wounded dog. Cheyenne caught a glimpse of his face.

It was white, and the moustache showed up as a trim, black inverted U over a pathetically dropping mouth. A deathly white face, with fear and surprise written on it. And death there, too.

Coltnus got into the middle of the corridor then collapsed. Cheyenne waited. Gauerke didn't come out. The place was very silent save for the hum of a distant electricity generator.

After a minute, Cheyenne ran down to Coltnus. He was bending over the man when he heard sounds along by the stairway. The G-man looked round, but there was no one in sight. He stooped, grabbed Coltnus and dragged him into the physiotherapy department. He didn't switch on the light; sufficient came in from the corridor through the frosted glass door-window.

Coltnus was in a bad way. He had been shot four times through the body. You don't shoot a man so many times in the places where Coltnus had taken the lead without them being deliberate. These were placed shots, designed to hurt before Coltnus died. It was the act of a vicious, savage slayer.

Coltnus was nearly out of the world.

Cheyenne said, softly, 'What happened? You fall out with Gauerke?'

Coltnus didn't recognise him. But he

spoke . . . he wanted to speak. He was a coward and couldn't die quietly.

And yet his first whispered words were of bewilderment. 'I . . . didn't think he'd dare show up. Not with Russ and the boys against him.'

That was news. Gauerke's gang had turned against him. The cripple had guts, coming here alone to face up to them. But then a man who built railroads in the old days of the roaring west must have a lot of sand even in a crippled body.

'Why was Russ against him?' prompted Cheyenne. Coltnus was dimming out of life rapidly.

Coltnus stirred. That bewilderment came back to his eyes. 'It seemed easy . . . we thought we'd make the kidnapping real . . . '

'You double-crossed the old man?' Cheyenne could see it now, could understand what had puzzled Joe Hencke who had spoken of some underlying worry attached to that ransom note that Gauerke had received.

The gang must have seen an easy way of getting a hundred grand out of the millionaire . . . just a nice, sweet double-cross on the old man. And by the look of things, Henry Coltnus had been in on the scheme to make the kidnapping real.

'Yes.' Cheyenne had to bend low over the dying man to hear him. 'It seemed so easy. I thought . . . it would make me in strong with the boys.'

'You wanted to run the gang yourself?' Cheyenne had met a lot of amateurs like that in his time, all with secret hankerings to be big, tough mobster leaders. Always they wanted to be the big shot, never the guys who did the running around.

'Yes.' It didn't seem much of an ambition to Coltnus now. 'It was my idea. Only . . . Gauerke came back. He's a devil.'

'What's he doing mixed up in gang warfare?' Cheyenne didn't think the fellow would last more than a few seconds. There was blood trickling out of his mouth now, and his eyes were glazing. He was dying; there was nothing Cheyenne could do to stop the end. But Coltnus might say something useful in his last moments.

'Lou Barce tried to pull a protection stunt

on Gauerke's fridge freighters . . . Gauerke went out to exterminate him . . . it gave . . . idea . . . run a mob for the hell of it. Gauerke had been respectable too long, I guess . . . '

There was too much blood suddenly in Coltnus' mouth. He went on living a few minutes longer, but he couldn't say much more that Cheyenne understood.

Still, he'd thrown light on the situation. A rough and tough old millionaire threatened by mobsters. He fights back the way he's always fought . . . with their own weapons. He hires a mob of professional gunnies . . . then, for the hell of it, decides to run out the big mobs and take over their rackets. Yes, that would be the sort of thing an old hellion like Gauerke would do.

Ambitious, cocky Henry Coltnus, his private medical adviser, had joined him. But he'd been too smart. He thought to turn the mob against the old man, and clear a hundred grand in the process. Only the ruthless old man had boldly returned to blast all ambition out of Coltnus' life.

Cheyenne was getting up off his knees, those dying eyes trying to hold him in focus. Coltnus seemed to be trying to say, 'Chair! Chair!' But it might have been some other word.

The special agent paused, not quite erect. He was suddenly tense, rigid.

There was a draught playing on his neck. The door behind him was furtively opening. *Someone knew he was in that room*.

Cheyenne's gun jumped into his hand and he wheeled. Three people were coming through that door. One was a stranger.

The first man was . . . Paul Zaharias.

The next person . . . October Raine.

October whispered, 'For Pete's sake don't pull that trigger!' Then she flew into his arms.

Cheyenne sighed his relief, then asked the obvious thing. 'How on Earth did you get aboard?' He hadn't heard that elevator operate since Gauerke's arrival, and if it had been used he would have heard it for certain.

Paul whispered, 'We came out on a fire

float. We came off an extension ladder as we passed the bubble.'

'That's great. Now we can do something.'

Then October told how they had traced him there.

'I had an awful moment when I was doing that moll act,' she told him. 'I kept hearing a kid outside shouting a special edition. I thought once I even heard him shout the name of Red Heydendahl. Suddenly I remembered something that Joe Hencke had said to me the previous night when I went across to his table . . . he'd just been making an editor eat worms.'

Paul broke in, 'A smart newspaper editor had given Joe hell when it seemed that you'd been killed and Red had got away. So, when you were safely out of the mob's hands, Joe went and told that editor the truth. Today, of course, it came out on the streets.'

'I beat it out of the office,' October went on. 'I guessed I might be more useful out of range of their guns when the fun began. I phoned Joe Hencke. He's a good guy. He sent Paul and Jim Chew here to help me. We followed when you went to Hahn's apartment. I couldn't warn you.'

'Did you try to phone me?'

'How could I? People don't go around asking for Red Heydendahl, do they?'

Paul took up the tale. 'We then followed you out to that 'florists', then across to the morticians'. We lost you after that. We saw Hanky Hahn come away alone. We waited for hours, but you didn't show up.'

October whispered, 'You big lug, it was awful, wondering what had happened to you in that death parlour.'

'Did you see the casket get taken out?' They nodded. He grinned. 'You didn't know I was inside?'

'Not until later. When we got tired Paul and Jim went up to that mortician and did a tough-talking act. He was too scared of Hahn to talk at first, but in time he got to be even more scared of the F.B.I. and he told us where you'd been taken. The problem after that was how to get aboard without spoiling any of your plans.'

'There's a big tough mob aboard this Glass Bubble,' Cheyenne said, 'We can't tackle 'em by ourselves. Can we get help any way?'

Paul told him, 'That's all fixed. Joe Hencke's got a squad moored back along the shore. If we want them we have to signal.'

The special agent smiled with satisfaction. 'Go signal 'em in right away,' he told them. 'Send the elevator down so they can come up easily.'

Jim Chew nodded and went quietly back into the corridor. The others crossed to the observation bay and looked out.

In the distance they heard the whine of the elevator. Looking down they saw the yellow glow as it descended to the landing pontoons. The elevator door opened, and light flooded on to the staging; someone stepped out and a light blinked on and off towards where Joe Hencke was waiting.

Then all three wheeled as a door opened down the corridor and they heard the hysterical voice of Dilys Gauerke. She was struggling to get out of the room, but Norm Gauerke had his big hands on her, so that as they came out she was dragging him with her.

Gauerke was shouting with passion, though they couldn't distinguish what he was saying. Then clearly they heard his daughter shout hysterically, 'You shot him like a dog. He didn't have a chance. Oh, you swine, you cold-blooded swine.'

Somehow she dragged herself away, but the force of it flung her back against the wall and she fell in a huddle against it.

Gauerke snarled, 'Pull yourself together. Don't you know which side your bread's buttered? It's done now, isn't it? Get that man of mine and let's get off this bubble before those hoods see me. Come on; do as you're told!' He was a man who believed in having people do as he wanted.

But he seemed to have gone too far with the girl. She swayed to her feet, her face white. 'I've had enough of you. You're a beast and you've always been a beast. I won't fetch your man . . . I'll fetch a gun!'

And then she went hysterical again. 'I'll kill you, I tell you! You're not fit to live! I loved Henry and that's why you killed him as you did!'

They saw the fury on Gauerke's face at

that passionate declaration, and then he started to pull his chair round so that he was directly facing the girl.

What happened next wasn't quite understandable. All in a fraction of a second the girl stopped shrieking threats and instead went into a whale of a panic. As if she could see some menace in the cripple that was lost on them, she began to retreat, her voice echoing over and over again, 'Oh, God, no . . . don't! Have mercy on me! Don't, don't!'

Then she turned and went down the corridor like the wind. Cheyenne saw the cripple pull his chair round as if to go after her, but it wedged against the corridor wall, and then they heard him growl as much as to say, 'Aw, hell, let her go!'

Cheyenne stepped out into the corridor. October and Paul came close behind. Gauerke caught the movement out of his eye corner and whipped his chair round like lightning.

Cheyenne said, 'I'm going to take you with me.'

Gauerke's smile switched on. And the smile was genuine. He said, heartily, 'I couldn't wish for a better escort. You're just in time . . . any moment now I reckon things are going to open up.'

'They are.' Cheyenne nodded. 'Maybe we'd be better right along by the elevator . . . I'm expecting friends that way.'

Gauerke inclined his head. He was a cool customer.

They began to move down the corridor. Cheyenne told him, 'When we get ashore I'm going to hold you on a charge of murder!'

'Murder? That's a serious crime, isn't it?' Gauerke was mocking, his smile growing like an early morning sun. 'Give a name to the corpse, will you?'

'Henry Coltnus.'

'I didn't shoot him.'

'I didn't say he was shot.'

'How else could a cripple kill a healthy young man? If you tell me he's dead and then accuse me of killing him, I guess the answer must be he's been found with a bullet in him.'

'Bullets,' corrected Cheyenne gently. They were by the elevator now.

Gauerke gave his big Japanese smile.

'But I don't carry a gun. Search me.'

Paul looked at the special agent. Cheyenne nodded. They had nothing else to do. Paul made a thorough search, then shook his head. There was no gun on him; neither was there one hidden in the rugs wrapped around him.

'He is unarmed,' said Paul emphatically, and Cheyenne knew he wasn't mistaken.

It rocked him, because he'd been certain that the murder gun would be on the cripple. Surely a man like Gauerke wouldn't wander around a boat full of double-crossing mobsters without carrying a weapon. Yet that appeared to be the case.

On an impulse he went back to the room that Gauerke had just left. It was vital that if a charge were to be made against the millionaire the murder weapon should be found. He found himself in an office that was as well-furnished as a lounge. There was a big polished desk over to one side, with chairs drawn to it as though Coltnus and Dilys Gauerke had been dining when the millionaire came bursting in on them. The remains of the meal were on a tray on the desk.

Cheyenne made a lightning search. There was blood across the carpet to show of the crime, but no trace of the gun. Cheyenne looked at the ports, screwed down because of the air-conditioning aboard, and knew that the weapon hadn't been disposed of that way.

He went back to the elevator. Gauerke was mocking him with his big smile. 'You didn't find anything?'

Cheyenne shook his head. 'You're goin' to be held anyway, Gauerke,' he told him. 'We can fix a lot of charges on you while we get around to persuading your daughter to give evidence against you.'

'My daughter's evidence would not be admissible in court against her father.' He was smart, Norm Gauerke.

But not smart enough.

Cheyenne said, softly, 'Except that she isn't your daughter.'

It was a guess, a pure blind guess, inspired by the passion in the girl's words as she had stormed at Gauerke. Then triumph swept over him. For a fraction of a second the millionaire's big smile started to go. He corrected it too late.

Cheyenne said, softly, 'We can check up. We'll be able to prove she's known as your daughter only to make your liaison unknown among your respectable friends. She's not your daughter, and she'll talk against you.'

'The damn' tramp,' snarled Gauerke, but there was cunning on his face. He started to pull his chair round to face them, but at that second they heard the throb-throb of an approaching launch. Cheyenne and the girl crossed to an observation bay, leaving Paul Zaharias to keep watch on Gauerke. Paul could do that all right. He was a very smart young G-man.

They were too near to the elevator to see the stage completely below, but they saw a dim shadow of a boat without lights come slowly bumping against the protective fenders. Then someone came jumping quickly on to the landing stage.

October suddenly gripped Cheyenne by the arm. 'What was that?'

There had been a sudden cry from below, followed by the sound of something heavy plunging into the water. Like a body falling in.

The elevator started to whine as it ascended. Pressing against the glass, Cheyenne saw something go quickly past the Glass Bubble, caught in the swift-moving shore current. Whoever it was began to pick up stroke and then swim strongly as he faded into the night.

Then they heard a shout from out in the lake. They couldn't distinguish the words, but October knew the voice.

'Jim!' she exclaimed horrified. 'That was Jim Chew, who came out with us!'

'Something's gone wrong.' The thought raced through Cheyenne's brain. G-man Jim Crew had been tossed into the lake . . . and probably bumped on the head before that was done to him.

'This can't be Joe Hencke and the boys,' he rapped.

'Then who . . . ?' began a bewildered October.

But Cheyenne knew and was racing across to the elevator entrance. It was just rising level with the floor.

Hanky Hahn and a dozen mobsters were crowded inside.

9

Gauerke's last grin

Cheyenne knew it would be Hahn before he saw him. He'd guessed what had happened. Jim Chew had signalled to the boats at the shore jetty, and Hahn had been cruising by and seen it and thought it was the signal Cheyenne had arranged to send to them.

They had come gliding in ahead of the Fed launches. Now they were aboard the Glass Bubble.

Cheyenne shouted, 'Move, Paul!' and held open a door that led into a remedial gymnasium. He switched on and flooded the big, well-equipped gym with light. There were doors opposite. That was satisfying, and he stood to one side as Paul came pelting in with the cripple in his wheelchair. Gauerke wasn't grinning now. This was something he didn't understand. But he didn't like it.

Paul didn't understand it, either, and Cheyenne shouted across . . . 'It's Hanky Hahn's gang come aboard. They're here to beat hell outa Russ Amann and the boys . . . and me, I guess.'

'But not me.' The thought put a grin back on that big, beefy face.

'Not,' said Cheyenne, 'unless I tell 'em you're the big boss, the guy that's cost 'em plenty dough.'

They got through the far doors and onto a plain passageway that was clearly where the workers aboard the Glass Bubble lived. As Cheyenne ran after the wheelchair someone came into the gym behind them and opened up with an automatic.

Cheyenne made a jump for the door, then stood to one side and clipped back two snapshots. It made Hank Hahn's gunnie think. He went back through those doors so quickly he tripped and landed on his neck. Another hood shoved his gun through. Cheyenne smashed the glass where he thought the guy might be keeping his head, but it seemed the fellar was wise and was crouching. He just took his hand out of danger, and the gun disappeared.

Paul called back, 'They'll be running round the corridors to find another way to get us.'

The shooting had stirred up interest on the bubble. Some greasy apes climbed the steel ladder from the power plant and went back to their jobs as if they loved them.

A long-tailed waiter tripped prettily round the corner, tapping his cissy fingertips together with vexation at the noise. He saw Paul galloping down with a gun, and promptly penguined off in a hurry back to the dining room.

Cheyenne knew it was the dining room they were approaching because the smell of food was growing stronger. He shouted to Paul. 'Watch out, Paul! The Amann mob's along there!'

He banged the wheelchair through some swing doors, and Paul turned and ran in after them. Cheyenne said, 'Let's do without lights.'

They stood within the place and that hot, steamy, smell of Turkish baths assailed them. They began to perspire. Then their eyes got used to the light that came in from either end of the room, from the lighted corridors beyond the glass-panelled swing doors.

They sat on a padded stomach bench . . . the one the masseurs used when they were slapping the weight off the middle of their over-laden patrons. Gauerke was silent, watching them, listening.

Paul whispered, 'Look, when Joe Hencke arrives he'll be stymied . . . that elevator's up top now.'

'Yeah.' Cheyenne thought for a moment. 'One of us will have to go back and somehow get the elevator down to the landing stage. And I reckon Hank will have a guard on it to cover his retreat.'

October breathed, 'Sssh!'

A shadow had flitted across the glass of the door leading out to the passageway. Then another went by, and then another.

Cheyenne said, 'That's the Amann mob your old hucksters, Gauerke. For why? They've none of 'em got hats on, like men who have just been sitting down to eat. The Hahn gang will be wearing hats, because they've just come from outside.'

'So now we've got the Hahn mob prowling after us down one corridor, while Russ Amann and boyfriends stalk us along the passage. Now I know what they mean by encirclement,' October said thoughtfully.

'Do you?' whispered Cheyenne, and shoved his arm around her slim waist. She cuddled up to him and they all stood still, waiting.

Still there was no disturbance from either the passage or the corridor. Cheyenne at length sighed. 'I guess I'd better do some scouting. I reckon they're going carefully into the rooms along the corridor; give 'em time and they'll find us. I want to get to the elevator, so we can bring up reinforcements when we need 'em.'

He went away quickly. Apparently he found a door leading into a side room, and he went through that. Little more than a minute later he came gliding quietly back to them.

'You can get through a series of rooms

. . . hot chambers, I guess . . . that way, and then get out on to the corridor quite near the elevator.'

'And what's along that corridor?' . . . Paul.

'Hanky Hahn and half a dozen of his mob. They're going through the rooms, trying to dig us out. When I looked out they'd found Coltnus' body and that was puzzling them more than somewhat.'

'How many are at the elevator?'

'I'd say maybe four or five . . . might even be six. But three of 'em are down along from it, guarding it from attack the opposite way.'

'The way Russ Amann will come?'

'If that was Russ and his boys,' nodded Cheyenne, looking towards the passage door. 'But we must get to that elevator first. We must be there before Joe Hencke's launches arrive . . . they won't be able to do a damned thing unless we get the elevator to them.'

October hissed, 'Move, you two. I can hear 'em out in the corridor. Looks like this is the next place for search!'

Paul threw his weight on to the chair

and sent it spinning through the narrow doorway that Cheyenne opened up for him . . . there was a moment when the chair stuck, and Gauerke at once started cursing. It was evident that the big shot didn't like the idea of being caught by either Russ Amann or the mob he had tried to gun out of business . . . Hahn's gunnies.

It brought the remark to Paul's lips; 'What the heck! Why are we shoving this guy around? Why don't we beat it on our own and leave the guy to take his chances?'

Cheyenne said, shortly, 'He's my prisoner. I don't let go of my prisoners. I want him alive, so that he can stand his charges for the murder of Henry Coltnus, if nothing else.'

Gauerke grinned contemptuously, 'You'll never pin that on to me, copper. I got too much money says you can't do it. Did you find the gun?' he jeered.

'One thing you forget, Gauerke,' Cheyenne told him. 'I'm a witness to the fact that the dying man told me you'd killed him . . . and if I come out of this alive I'll take care you don't silence your former girlfriend, Daughter Dilys.'

October saw the evil on that face and thought: Jeez, if Gauerke had a gun, I guess he'd blow Cheyenne's head off. Right now he could murder him!

She got behind Cheyenne as he helped shove the chair through the last of the rooms; whispered, 'For Pete's sake take no chances with Gauerke. I saw murder in his face. And remember, G-man, if he can dispose of you he'll have destroyed the principal . . . perhaps the only — witness that can testify against him with regard to this Coltnus crime.'

She heard Cheyenne whisper, 'I'll watch out,' then he hurried ahead to open the door leading out on to the corridor. He had taken the precaution of relocking it from inside, so that it could not be opened from the corridor, and now they watched anxiously as he pulled the door open a crack to peer out.

It was at this moment that they heard furtive sounds behind them. Cheyenne beckoned. 'There's an observation bay a few yards along and bang against the elevator shaft. We're going to rush it, get the elevator down for when Joe Hencke arrives, then hold the mob back from the elevator as long as we can.'

Paul began to whisper, but what he was saying became lost in the tornado of sound that suddenly developed throughout the bubble.

One solitary shot rang out, starting the whole thing off. A couple of seconds later it sounded like a war had started. A tremendous fusillade of revolver fire developed, and the bedlam was intensified by the echo along the long passageway.

Paul shouted above the din, 'The gangs have met head on!' Then they heard him shout again, 'It won't last long. Chicago gun-battles never do. They'll blaze away then run for it.'

So Cheyenne threw open the door, just as the screaming developed among the women guests of the Glass Bubble away at the dining room end of the corridor. The noise was terrific, but it helped to cover their movements.

They went head down, in a fine flurry

of movement, and were almost across when one of the tense, nervous guards at the elevator head saw them. He opened fire, but both Paul Zaharias and Cheyenne ripped off as he turned his gun towards them. The gunnie . . . it looked like the hophead to Cheyenne . . . gasped with pain, then for some reason began stumbling along towards where a passage entered on the corridor. Someone took a quick pot at him round the corner, and the hophead went down groaning.

There was only another man at the elevator: they could see now that the others had moved along the corridor and were covering the passage-end from the doorways.

Cheyenne turned his gun on the hood, and that wise guy promptly leapt for the shelter of a doorway along with a comrade. Cheyenne let the chair hurtle into the bay under its own momentum, then hurtled across to the elevator. Paul went down on one knee and covered him with brisk fire that sent the startled hoods back into their doorways.

The G-man clawed his hand through to

the operator's lever inside . . . it wasn't the kind that could be sent down with a touch of a button from a panel alongside the gate. The elevator started moving, and Cheyenne pulled his hand back through the gate just in time.

He started to turn, thinking, 'So far so good. Now we must cover that elevator until Joe Hencke arrives to round up these mobs.'

Then Paul ran out of ammunition. The hoods came out from their holes at the silence and blasted away. Cheyenne took the skin off his side in a long baseball slide to beat the bullets.

But he got home safe, and that was all that mattered.

He was sitting up, when a dazzling white beam hit them on the back of their heads. October turned and looked out over the lake. Three launches were tearing in towards them, and the powerful spotlight up for'ard told them they were police boats.

'They must have heard the commotion and they're racing up to our rescue,' called October. 'Hold on another couple of minutes and they'll be here.'

'Yeah . . . but Hanky Hahn's seen those lights and he knows what it means. He'll be desperate to get to his boat before the boys arrive.'

'Any moment now Russ Amann's going to tumble to it, too,' Paul said. 'Then that'll be two mobs desperate to get off the bubble . . . rats trying to get off the ship.'

Cheyenne prayed, 'Oh, God, if only we can hold out! What a prize, to pull in a murderer and a couple of top-line Chicago mobs!'

Hanky Hahn himself came charging down the corridor. Cheyenne saw those long dirty teeth and tried to knock them out with a bullet. It must have been very near, for abruptly Hahn spun into a doorway. The rest of his mob came creeping up along the walls, dodging from doorway to doorway, their guns putting up such a fury of fire that Paul and Cheyenne had to keep back under cover. The screaming from the other end of the bubble was like nothing they'd ever heard before.

Then the rest of Hanky Hahn's men

started to double back towards the elevator, only they had to fire two ways at once. For Russ Amann's mob was pouring out of the passage end, and it was obvious that they, too, were making a desperate bid to get quickly to the elevator head.

Cheyenne was firing when he could, and then he began to realise that Paul was shouting to him. Then Paul came and pulled him back out of danger. For some reason the G-man was grinning.

Cheyenne, filled with the lust of battle, shouted above the roaring confusion, 'What the hell, Paul!'

But Paul Zaharias just grinned and shouted back, 'Hold your fire, Chey. Just watch this; it's goin' to be funny.'

And then Cheyenne got it, saw what he was driving at.

Both gangs wanted to get to that elevator first. Both were approaching it but from opposite ends of a long corridor. So now they were belting hell out of each other, each determined not to let the other get to the elevator at all.

'Dog eat dog,' chortled Paul Zaharias, delighted.

'Stalemate,' Cheyenne shouted. But October wasn't saying anything.

She was puzzling over something. She'd caught a movement out of the corner of her eye, but now she was beginning to look for it. She couldn't understand it.

Big, bald, beefy Gauerke was manoeuvring that wheelchair curiously. As Cheyenne moved from one side of the observation bay to the other, October began to notice that Gauerke, a strange look of concentration on his face, each time began to turn the chair so that it was always facing, or nearly facing, the G-man. Though it seemed to October that no sooner did Gauerke get to be exactly facing the detective than Cheyenne would shift his position so that the tracking operation had to be resumed.

It puzzled October, watching. She could see that Gauerke was in deadly earnest in his manoeuvring, whatever lay behind it, because his lips were drawn back in a snarl of concentration, and each time Cheyenne moved a hiss of annoyance came from him.

She looked up . . . and saw something else. The door down the corridor . . . the one they'd come through . . . was beginning to open. She was about to shout a warning when she realised that Dilys Gauerke . . . she still thought of her by that name . . . was coming through.

She thought: The girl's trying to join us; she must be terrified of all this shooting.

Then she saw that the girl held an automatic in her hand. She realised that Dilys Gauerke's blazing eyes were fixed on the man whose name she had adopted. But Norm Gauerke wasn't looking at her. These was a look of satisfaction just creeping onto his face, the beginnings of the celebrated Gauerke grin began to grow.

For Cheyenne was standing still now, and he, Gauerke, was exactly in the position that he had manoeuvred for this last minute or so. His hand moved.

Dilys Gauerke's voice screamed above the rattle of guns. 'Watch out, G-man!'

Cheyenne whirled. Saw the grin on Gauerke's face, and immediately on an instinct began to throw himself down to the ground. As he was falling he saw Gauerke's hand touch some part of the armrest of his chair. The end of the armrest dropped and Cheyenne saw the muzzle of a revolver. Then Gauerke touched a brass stud on the upholstery of the arm, and the gun blazed into life.

It missed Cheyenne, but Dilys Gauerke didn't miss the millionaire.

October saw her hand come up. Whether she was trying for revenge or was doing it to save the G-man's life they never knew. Her gun came up, she fired . . . and Norm Gauerke had grinned his last grin.

When they looked at him he was slumped in his chair, a hole appearing just over the right eye. October shuddered, and Cheyenne went to her. She whispered, 'Oh, Charlie, you nearly died on me that time!'

Cheyenne was looking with interest at the gun mechanism hidden within that padded armrest. 'Neat,' he murmured, 'So that's how he killed Henry Coltnus . . . and Dilys Gauerke saw him do it and so knew the significance of any manoeuvring with the chair.' He was thinking back to that moment when the girl had fled in terror because Gauerke had tried to pull the chair round to face her. He didn't know of the manoeuvring that had taken place behind his own back . . . only October had seen that.

They looked across at Dilys Gauerke. She had slumped to the floor just within the doorway, but she didn't seem to be hurt. She just looked pale and washed out and very dull, as if suddenly she'd had enough of excitement.

The battle had one last, final flare-up. Hahn won through to the elevator head, beating back Russ Amann and his mob to do it.

But it didn't do him any good. Maybe that was why Cheyenne watched him without shooting him down, though he could have done so from around the corner of the bay.

Because that elevator was whining now as it ascended, and Cheyenne was willing to bet that this was Joe Hencke with a squad carrying sub-machine-guns.

It was. Hank Hahn saw the car full of G-men. He snarled and started to lift his gun to blow then out of existence, though they'd have got him before he had finished the lot off. Cheyenne's finger tightened on the trigger . . . then relaxed as Hahn threw down his gun in disgust.

Hahn's mob saw the squad and immediately began to heave their artillery through broken windows. Russ Amann caught on and unloaded his weapons the same way himself.

When Joe Hencke stepped out from that elevator, machinegun cocked ready, there wasn't any fighting going on . . . there wasn't a shot being fired and he couldn't have found a gun on that deck if he'd tried.

The two gangs weren't exactly fraternizing, but they were both putting on an act of bewildered innocence.

Hahn set the note with his greeting old Joe Hencke. 'You wouldn't believe,' he complained. 'I got nerves, so I came see if they could rest me up on the bubble for a while. I just arrived with friends, when, hell, if someone didn't start firing off a gun.'

Hencke said, frostily, 'It's a good story at short notice.'

The camel-faced Hahn snarled, 'It's the one my attorney will give you.'

Then Russ Amann was shoved forward, hand reaching for the ceiling lights. He started in about being aboard for his health. Cheyenne said. 'We got a place much better for your kind of troubles, Russ. Shove 'em in a cell, Joe, and take no notice of 'em.'

He stood aside and watched as they took the bad-tempered, sullen mobsters down to the landing stage in batches. October came across to say that Dilys Gauerke was all right; just suffering from shock.

'I tried to help her. I told her there'd be no bother over killing Guaerke because it saved your life. That right, Charlie?'

'I suppose so.' Cheyenne wasn't bothered. The girl was only small fry in the gang, anyway, and she seemed to have suffered at the hands of the millionaire. 'Reckon we'll just keep quiet about the shooting.'

When the last of the mobsters was showed below, Cheyenne walked across to his brother inspector, Joe Hencke. Joe was grinning at him.

'Some vacation you got for yourself, Charlie!'

'Sure,' said Cheyenne. 'Now, I reckon to finish the vacation with a nice tour that'll embrace Yellowstone Park.'

Hencke was shaking his head.

'No? Why not?'

'Because L.A. office came through this afternoon to say there was no vacation for Charlie Chey. They reckoned they'd got a nice new murder case waiting for him to solve out at Oakland. Your orders are to catch the first plane back.'

Cheyenne said, 'Blast,' and he thought he heard an echo to the word. He realised that October was indulging in unladylike language again.

Then she wailed, 'Why did I have to fall for a G-man? I share him with crooks and daffy millionaires and a lot of other G-men, and not even on a vacation do I get him to myself.'

Joe Hencke breathed, 'Honey, you could have me all the time.' And he might have been serious at that.

Cheyenne tucked the girl's arm under his own. Said, 'Baby doesn't want you.

Baby loves me, don't you, honey?'

They got into the elevator.

When they were down far enough not to be seen, Cheyenne slipped his arms round her and said, 'Like to finish your vacation helping me on this nice murder case out at Oakland?'

She said, 'No,' pouting.

He kissed her.

She sighed and said, 'That's another . . . girl changed her mind, I reckon. Okay, G-man, let's go on this other case.'

THE END

Other titles in the
Linford Mystery Library:

THE EMPTY COFFINS

John Russell Fearn

Two gruesome murders were discovered in the village of Little Payling. The bodies of a farmer and a local builder had been drained of blood. Their necks bore deep wounds, which centred on their jugular veins. When Scotland Yard arrived they made little progress — until Peter Malden became suspicious about his wife Elsie's first husband George Timperley, who had committed suicide. Then Elsie herself died and was buried — but her coffin, like George Timperley's, was found to be empty!

POISON IVY

Gordon Landsborough

'She's death to men,' they told trouble-buster Joe P. Heggy. And when he knew her past . . . the men who'd died for her . . . he tried to keep clear. But she wouldn't let him. Then, when a mob formed a manhunt, they became the targets — their lives were at stake, because of the fears and jealousy of a craven power-seeker. They endured a night of fear in the mountains as they battled to survive, and Heggy learned what made her Poison Ivy.

THE SECRET FILES OF SHERLOCK HOLMES

Gary Lovisi

The Adventure of the Missing Detective: Whilst travelling incognito in Switzerland, Sherlock Holmes is shocked almost beyond belief to discover that Queen Victoria is dead — and that his old nemesis, Professor James Moriarty, had not only survived their confrontation at the Reichenbach Falls, but had been knighted and appointed personal advisor to the new heir! Meanwhile, *The American Adventure* provides a fascinating insight into Holmes' earlier life when, during his travels with Dr. Joseph Bell, he was tutored in the art of deduction by the master . . .